APOLLO: *UNLEASHED!*

The Cavanaugh Series

JC Wardon

Mystic Waters Books
JC Wardon

Mystic Waters Books
JC Wardon

APOLLO: UNLEASHED!
Copyright © 2015, JC Wardon
Trade Paperback ISBN: 978-1-944454-92-0

Editor, Gilly Wright
Cover Art Design by Calliope-Designs.com

Digital Release, 2015
Trade Paperback Release, March 2016

Media > Books > Fiction > Romance Novels
Categories: Witch, Psychic, Telepathy, Humor

This print edition is published by author/owner JC Wardon, Mystic Waters Books

JC Wardon
www.jcwardon.com

APOLLO: *Unleashed!*

Will unleashing his magic liberate his imprisoned heart as well?

Dangerous situations suit firefighter Apollo Cavanaugh-Whitehawk just fine. Born second in an identical set of mystical triplets, he chooses to rely on his purely human abilities. Life is complicated enough with all the magic and mayhem his family causes in Mystic Waters....

But... When a beautiful woman arrives in mortal danger, who has mystical abilities of her own, he finds the leash he's put on himself, may need to be released if he has any chance of keeping her alive!

Chapter One

Apollo Cavanaugh-Whitehawk swung the hatchet, slicing deep into the short length of wood he'd cut from the much longer log of a downed tree. He bent down to lift the two pieces and threw them over where he'd soon stack the building pile. He'd been at it all morning, knowing there was no hurry to prepare for the still distant upcoming winter, but it was something to do now that he had so much time on his hands.

The subtle breeze blowing through the branches overhead shifted, and the sweetness of Mystic Mountain altered and took on an injurious smell. He halted in the process of lifting another cord to chop and tilted his face upward, lifting his nose toward the pristine sky, surprised and a little befuddled by the odd smell. Though the massive pines around his cabin blocked out a good deal of the sun's light, enough beamed through in the small clearing to reveal both a cloudless sky and the a hint of dark gray smoke which was now sucking at his lungs. A chill went up his sweaty spine and hardened the nipples on his equally glistening chest.

There was a moment of hesitation, but only that,

before he took off in the direction of the increasingly thickening smoke. He hadn't brought his cell phone out to the cabin, which was basically useless anyway on the mountain, but it had a built-in walky-talky feature that worked just fine and always alerted him when any kind of emergency broke out in Mystic Waters. He hadn't meant to leave it behind at the station, or that's what he been telling himself since seeking the solitude of his isolated cabin. He was on an official vacation for the next two weeks from the search and rescue unit of their fire department, because he needed to take a break.

A real one.

Where no one and nothing touched him.

The once quiet mountain was becoming a hotbed of disasters, and his job was taking a toll. Both physically and mentally. The latter his greatest concern, and if he was being honest, it wasn't just the job.

Too many strange things were happening in Mystic Waters. Perhaps all over the world. Although most people would think his family strange to start with, he knew each to be harmless unless provoked into defensive mode. No, it wasn't that the surrounding area was filled to the brim with a multitude of mystics wielding different kinds of magic. It was something else... Something *evil*. And the weight of it all, piled on over the last couple of years, was what had sent him into seclusion. Which was where he really wanted to stay today!

Instead, he was being forced to change his plans from an afternoon filled with cold beers and mindless hard work, aka *hiding out*, so he could see just what kind of trouble someone had gotten into.

There was no choice. Regardless of the intrusion on his own life, he wasn't built to ignore someone in need. It made no difference their actions usually caused the disaster from which they needed rescuing, or that the sour mood he'd awakened with told him to let someone else handle whatever had happened. He was who he was, and he had to respond.

Having no idea how far up the mountain he'd be required to run, and wanting to nip this problem in the bud as quickly as possible, Apollo did something he'd avoided for the past several years. He called upon the speed of the wind, his granted mystical gift acquired during the *ascending* when he'd turned fifteen years old.

His booted feet barely touched the rough terrain and tangled vegetation as he sped toward the thickening smoke with nearly sonic speed. Since it took only seconds to reach the burning car, he had to stop abruptly and, as quickly assess the situation.

A young woman hung upside down in the overturned burning car, her frantic screams and pounding on the glass making her safety his first priority. Apollo placed his hand over his face and threw himself down on his stomach where he landed just beside the crushed driver's door. She looked at him with wide, terrified green eyes.

"Help me! Please!"

Apollo nodded. "Turn your face away!"

She did so immediately, and with his one hard fist to the window, the safety glass cracked and gave. He pulled the pieces away and looked inside as she turned back to him. "I'll get you. Just hold on!"

She nodded quickly, and he knew it was with hope more than assurance. He reached inside and fumbled with the latch of her belt buckle, until he found the button. He looked into her eyes, hoping the urgency within him wasn't reflected in his own eyes for her to see. He needed her confidence, or he was afraid she'd freak out and fight him. "I'm going to release your seatbelt and pull you out as you fall. I need you be completely limp. And I need you to trust me."

"Do it!" she screamed and then coughed harshly.

The weight of her on his arm was welcome, though he feared he was hurting her as he pulled her out with such haste. Once she was free of the seatbelt, which momentarily captured her right foot, he dragged her away, debating whether or not to lift her into his arms. All of his training said not to move such a victim, but he had no choice. The flames were getting bigger, and he was afraid the little car was about to explode.

"I'm sorry if I hurt you!" he shouted, when the flames turned to rolling roars. He lifted her with ease and sprinted backward away from the car. Apollo got nearly twenty feet before the explosion came, throwing metal and burning fiberglass their way. He turned away from the flying debris and lowered her to the ground so he could cover her body with his own.

She said nothing and didn't move, making Apollo fear he may have broken something within her the wreck hadn't. He placed her flat on her back and listened through the simple cotton dress as best he could for a heartbeat. He grasped her wrist and searched for a pulse. Getting nothing, he moved upward, placing his ear just above her lips, hoping for any signs of breath. He lost his own when her chest expanded suddenly, and rough coughing followed. Able to look into eyes that finally opened, he sighed his heartfelt relief.

Trembling as he never had before while under the duress of a rescue, Apollo sent her what he feared was a quivering smile.

"I'm trained to help you. Can you tell me your name?"

She coughed again, violently, eventually shaking her head slowly. Though that was disappointing, it was a relief she could move her head and not react in pain. His training had apparently deserted him. He should have secured her head and neck and demanded she lay still until he could find a way to get help.

She needed X-rays and possibly a CAT scan to determine if there was internal damage, though her lifting her arms and grabbing him with such strength likely negated an upper spinal injury. Unless adrenaline alone was holding her together.

"Get me away from here, please!"

"I can't until I'm sure you can be moved."

She shook her head, tears filling her eyes. "I'm fine. Nothing hurts *too* badly, but it hurts, so I know I can move."

"It's too dangerous," he countered. "Someone will see the smoke and come soon."

"No! We have to go now. The men who were following me, and bumped my car, will come back to make sure I'm dead. Please, get me out of here now!"

Apollo was too stunned to react, giving her the opportunity to roll out of his grip. He watched in disbelief as she jumped to her feet, and started to run. He hadn't realized how close to the mountainous road they were until just then. He looked back to see the fire in the trees and brush, and telepathed a message to his father, hoping that rusty skill still worked. He wished he could do the same with his mother, but Tom Whitehawk would have Mother Mountain take care of herself, and, once everyone else connected in the ways that they did, his mother and aunts would handle the fires quickly, and cleanse and restore the earth in a way no one would ever know an accident had happened.

He turned and took off at a run, catching up with the woman as she stumbled her way over roots, vines, and rocks. He pulled her to a stop, and forced her to face him.

"Who are you running from?"

She tried to pull free, but Apollo held her still. "Answer me. Who is trying to kill you?"

She licked her lips, and looked behind him in fear. When her gaze landed upon him again, there was resignation in the rise and fall of her shoulders.

"Men who want me, or want me dead. I can't say more. *Please!* We have to go. If they find you with me, they'll kill you too."

He wanted answers but knew they'd have to wait. With surprising strength she struggled against him again, and he was afraid she'd really hurt herself if he didn't do as she asked. "I'll carry you. I just need you to hold on, and close your eyes."

Indecision held her immobile before she nodded quickly and allowed him to lift her. Apollo waited until she did as told, and he took off at a fast run. As much as he wanted to pull upon the power of the wind again, he knew he'd have to rely on only athletic ability. Otherwise, he'd have to explain the unexplainable.

It took ten times as long to return to his cabin than it had to get to the disaster, but even that was faster than made sense to most people. He set her on her feet at his front door and quickly ushered her inside.

"Where am I?"

Apollo closed the door behind him, and turned to face her. "You're at my cabin."

"No, I mean, where am I? On a map."

He frowned. "Mystic Waters. West Virginia. Mystic Mountain, specifically. You didn't know?"

She shook her head, looking around the room as if afraid someone would jump out of the shadows. Her attention on him again, she almost smiled. "Your place is nice, but I have to get away from here. When they find the car, they'll find me."

"No. They won't."

The panic was returning, settling in her eyes.

"*Yes*, they will. We're too close. I have to go. Please!"

It took a moment of debate, but Apollo decided to tell her what little he could. "Your car, or what's left of it, is miles away down the mountain. No one will know where you are."

Shaking her head, she looked at him as if he was crazy.

"There's no way that's possible. We can't be that far away."

Apollo smiled, hoping it reassured. "We are. I can run very fast. I'll ask again, what's your name?"

Indecision was in her eyes, and flight, her stance. Apollo knew she was scared, and he was pushing, even if gently. "I don't care who you are, but I have to call you something."

She nodded with jerky movements. "Isabella."

"Okay, Isabella, you're safe here. I live deep in the forest. There is only one way to get to my cabin by automobile, and that's only if you know where to find the turn from the road, and it's camouflaged and not readily noticeable. No one but my family knows there is a cabin here."

The relief he expected to see wasn't there. If anything, she looked more concerned.

"Why would you live in such isolation?"

Apollo moved toward the kitchen and, as expected, she followed. "Do you need some water?"

Isabella nodded and stood back as he retrieved two of the bottles his cousins manufactured in the town below from the waterfalls of Mystic Mountain. Being a native son alone was a perk in Mystic Waters. His father's people were generously blessed with magic and were one with the land. And the magical land, in turn, was one with them. These waters replenished *all* who drank them, but, for his mystically infused Indian blood and the multi-cultural mystical blood of his mother's ancestors, the water offered even more.

She took a drink as did he, and they sighed together after swallowing. Zeus smiled at her, and she back at him, and something within him shifted. He looked away, and settled his bottle on the counter. "To answer your question, I like solitude when I'm not working."

She took another drink, and he could see its properties were settling within her. She was more relaxed, and the fear eased from her eyes. She seemed more curious than anxious now, as she glanced around. The kitchen and living room were one, with only the sofa separating them. The single bedroom was off to the right, and the bathroom took up the left wing. Both were as wide as the living room/kitchen as they held equal importance. The bedroom also accommodated the small office he'd set up, though he'd yet to use the small desk and chair. The bathroom, as were all the bathrooms his family designed, was fully tiled and held a shower that was a room itself, a sauna he rarely used unless to thaw his body after being out working for too many hours in frigid winter weather, and a plain white sink and toilet, all of which he was meticulous about cleaning.

He wasn't a germaphobe like some in his family, but he had high standards when it came to hygiene. And he could use a shower now. He looked over at Isabella and gauged her, relieved he had a little of his mother's ability to read people. She seemed content for the moment, but he still hadn't check her out.

"Do you hurt anywhere?"

Isabella's gaze flew his way, and her cheeks reddened, as if she'd been caught snooping. He grinned, thinking her cute.

"Just a little. But nothing to worry about. I actually feel pretty great, given the circumstances. But I need to get this smoke smell off me. I just don't have anything to change into." She crossed to the large window at the front of the cabin and looked out.

"You don't need to worry about anyone coming. I would know if they did."

She turned and lifted a brow at him. "You have a security system?"

Hoping the minute hesitation went unnoticed, Apollo nodded. His security system consisted of strong intuition and Lycanthrope, who would soon come to guard the area. His cousin, Sapphire, and her husband, the Lycanthrope Alpha, made sure their pack didn't let harm come to any under the Cavanaugh protection. And this woman, whoever she was, was now under his.

"I have clothes that will be too big for you, but you can shower and change into them until we can wash your dress. And I have female cousins who will bring some. They are all about your size, give or take." Apollo cringed. He had no idea if they were or not. Figuring it didn't matter, he shrugged.

Isabella bit her bottom lip, something he found endearing. His mother did that when she was working out a problem in her head, and he figured his new guest was doing the same.

"I'd love the shower and your clothes. But I don't want anyone else to know I'm here…for however long I'll be here."

The worry returned before she looked down at the floor.

"I have no idea where I'll go."

"You have time to figure that out. And you don't have to worry about my family. We protect people. They won't be rude and ask questions, at least not of you. If they ask me anything, I'll tell them to mind their own business." He grinned. "Nicely, of course.

"They won't say anything to anyone."

He'd almost told her they kept to themselves for the

most part outside of work, but he didn't want her to fear she'd stumbled into a creepy family of inbred hillbillies. He certainly couldn't tell her they did so to protect themselves, and each other, from discovery. There were those out there who sought people who held magic, and their purposes weren't always pure. The safest thing for everyone involved was to keep their magic to themselves.

"Come on into my bedroom, and we'll see what we can find. Then you can hit the shower, and I'll get one after."

She nodded and followed him, stopping just inside the large room. He went on to the dresser, giving her time to access her situation at her own pace. He knew the subject of sleeping arrangements would come up eventually, so he figured he'd give her a break and get it out of the way.

"The sofa turns into a full-sized bed."

He pulled out a T-shirt and shorts, thinking them her best bet. When he turned to her again, she was looking at him with tears teasing her lower lids. "Are you okay?"

She nodded and wiped at her eyes, leaving a streak of moisture across her cheek. "You're so nice. I don't know what to expect. But, thank you for all this."

He didn't expect to feel uncomfortable, but her gratitude was humbling. He shrugged. "It's nothing."

Her lips, trembling, lifted. "It's not nothing, right now, for me, it's *everything*. I'm without a home. Without any means to help myself. And I don't dare try to find either, even if I knew how to...."

Apollo wanted to ask questions, but there was time. She needed to trust him first, he understood that, and he had it to give. "I'm on vacation from work for the next couple of weeks. I'd be happy to help you, in any way you need. All you have to do it tell me what that is."

Isabella's eyes closed briefly, before she looked to him with confusion. "You're on...*vacation?*" She was very still for a moment, and then frowned as she looked around the room. "I'm sorry… I think that means I'm messing up your plans."

He found it odd that she made *vacation* sound as if he'd spoken it in a language foreign to her, but she was obviously traumatized by the wreck and whatever had preceded it. Apollo hoped to offer reassurance. "No plans. Just time off. You're actually keeping me from making busy work just to occupy my time."

She blew out a breath. "Are you sure?" At his nod, she reached out to take the clothing from his hands. Their fingers touched in the exchange, and their eyes met in surprise.

Apollo studied the sunburst fanning out from the center of her violet irises and found himself mesmerized and then a little drunk of a sudden. He was *certain* they'd been green before, but he had been in a panic to get her out of the car, and must have made an error.

But he didn't think so….

Not wanting her to know he felt as if the earth had shifted beneath his feet, Apollo bit back questions about before and focused on the now. "I've never seen eyes the color of yours."

She blinked rapidly before lowered her eyelids, making the long black lashes fan out to cover her eyes. Apollo tried not to take it personally, as he was sure that was not her intent. But the lost connection was another indication of her mistrust. He took a step back.

"I'll show you the bathroom."

He turned away, only to be stopped by her squeaky words.

"I'm special!"

He turned back, and looked her over. She was young, and amazingly beautiful, but he didn't know what she meant by *special*. "In what way?"

The fear was back in full force, and those eyes he'd studied now changed colors to a brighter green than before. He blinked but didn't react outwardly otherwise, although his insides were humming with an excitement he couldn't explain. He reached out to her without thinking, and she stepped back.

Apollo lowered his hand. "What are you?"

Her lips pressed together, and then she shrugged. "I'm not sure, exactly. I've been captive all my life. A science experiment, Sara said. All I know is I have certain abilities and others were always testing me. I figured out years ago they couldn't do what I do, but I didn't realize I was living in unusual circumstances until yesterday."

Not knowing where to start the questions popping in his head, Apollo focused on what he hoped was the simplest, "Who's Sara?"

"The woman who spent the last couple of years living with me." Isabella frowned. "Or I guess I spent them living with her. Until then, I'd never gotten to leave the big building I grew up in. She said I had to run away from the small farm we lived on or the people who held me were going to kill me so they could examine my brain and body. It wasn't until she took me to a gate I'd never seen before, leading off of what she said is the compound, that her words made sense."

Apollo mulled over her words, not sure if any of it made sense to him. Again focusing on the simplest, he asked, "How is it you knew how to drive?"

"Sara taught me after swearing me to secrecy. Until I escaped, I thought the town we lived down the road from was normal even though it only consisted of a handful of spread-out houses and a store, and the big building where I had to go every day to be tested. Over the last little while, Sara started making me drive once we were out of sight of those who watched our house, and we'd have to exchange places again before we got into the area close to town where people were likely to see us. It wasn't until I escaped that I saw how big the world really is."

Apollo tried to keep his expression neutral, but he was horrified. "How did you end up here?"

She shrugged. "I don't know. I just kept driving. Eventually I realized I was being followed, and when they got up next to me on this mountain, they put down their windows and shouted at me. I couldn't hear them, but I knew they wanted me to pull over. When I refused, they fell back and then rammed into the back of the car. Everything after that happened slowly, it seemed. The car took to the air and spun, and the next thing I know I hit the ground hard upside-down and the car starts to smell and smoke. I panicked, but I was so disoriented I couldn't think. It was only minutes before you were there, and now, here I am."

When Apollo said nothing, she rushed on. "I'm telling you the truth!"

He nodded, knowing what he was about to do was the one thing he'd sworn he never would again. "I believe you, and I'm going to tell you a truth not too many people outside of my family know, too. We have powers others don't understand as well. And you will be protected by us all."

She looked at him doubtfully, and Apollo smiled. "Put the clothes down and come with me. I'll show you."

Isabella did so instantly, and she followed him from the bedroom through the house and out the front door. Apollo knew he was taking a chance exposing himself to her, his family as well, but confidence she would bring them no harm wasn't just because he wanted to assure her of her own safety. Her spirit was pure, as indicated by the aura surrounding her. He waited until she was ready. "Watch this," he said, for the first time in a long time feeling pride about his gift. He walked to her left a few feet, ran around the house, and was instantly standing to the right of her.

Isabella's head swung around, and she gasped and then laughed. The musical sound lifted him from within, and he laughed too.

"You can transport yourself?" she asked in awe.

He shook his head. "No. I rounded the house. I told you I could run fast."

She looked at him in wonder. "That's amazing! What else can you do?"

Grinning, Apollo closed his eyes and called to the closest bird, the large eagle his father often indwelled when he wanted to soar. Brother Eagle's loud response was instant, and within a minute, he landed on Apollo's outstretched arm.

"Oh, my! He's beautiful!"

"Isabella, this is Brother Eagle, he too will watch over us to keep you safe."

Childlike wonder filled her eyes as she slowly approached, reminding Apollo how special the gifts he'd abandoned really were. It had been so long since he'd thought about the blessings of magic, he was a little in awe himself.

"Hi, Brother Eagle. Thank you." She looked to Apollo. "May I touch him?"

"He would like that."

She held out her hand, and Brother Eagle lowered his head. An almost serene expression entered her eyes when she smiled at Apollo. When she lowered her hand and stepped back, tears were again on her lower lashes, and this time, she allowed them to fall.

Apollo thanked the eagle and sent him on his way before he turned his attention to the woman-child who had so suddenly entered his life. "Why do you cry?"

At first she didn't answer, only stare into his eyes, and

then she moved forward and wrapped her arms around his bare chest. "Because I'm safe. I'm really safe."

Apollo held her loosely, not wanting to scare her by reacting to the confusing responses going on from within his body and, he feared, soon would be reflected, from without as well. With the line of work he'd chosen, with the horrors of the human wreckage he'd been called to handle, his mind and body were well trained to suppress reaction to all types of stimulation. But this was different.

He barely knew Isabella, had only been in her presence for less than half an hour, and his system was going crazy for her. It made no sense, except… *No!* Just because he'd used his gifts again didn't mean he'd be a slave to other aspects of the magic.

Apollo knew better than to think about a woman along those lines. *Especially* one so innocent. He'd only allowed himself to fall for a girl once, and even then, it hadn't felt like *this*. His one attempt at love, even *before* everything went sour, had just about ruined not only his own life, but had brought danger to the family he loved. To find himself captivated again now, with Isabella, was the last thing he needed.

She released him and stepped back, her face wet, her lips trembling. "I don't know how we found each other, but I'm so glad we did." She bit her bottom lip and chewed again for a time. "I have nothing to offer you in return for this place of safely, except myself."

Obligation wasn't he wanted from her. He didn't want anything at all from her…except to explore the feelings she evoked. Which he wouldn't do. "You owe me nothing. And never will."

She shook her head. "I owe you everything. And always will."

Her lips lifted. "But I guess we will both just have to live with that." Isabella's expression sobered. "I don't know how long it will take, or even have an idea how I can, but I will find a way to take care of myself eventually. I don't want depending on someone else to last forever. I've been caged all my life, even though I didn't know it until recently."

Isabella looked him over, a grin tugging at the lip she'd once again captured. "My name is Isabella Quinn, and I just realized, I've never asked yours."

Knowing he was in over his head when she smiled like that, he held out his hand. "Apollo. Apollo Whitehawk. It's so nice to meet you, Isabella Quinn."

Chapter Two

Isabella stood in the massive shower, both amused and somewhat confused by all the options. Several buttons and knobs controlled the different-sized showerheads, as well as how and from where they operated. She knew she was taking too long to simply get washed up, but she was free to explore according to Apollo, and that's exactly what she was going to do.

Once she settled on the ones she liked best, Isabella opened the bottle of shampoo, and instantly thought of the amazing fresh smells of the pristine mountainous air, *before* she'd filled it with smoke. The drive up the very green mountain, with her windows open, right before she realized she was being pursued and closed them, was so sweet she'd actually thought she'd found how Sara explained Heaven. That short reprieve from the anxiety she'd carried for hundreds of miles was short lived, though.

Isabella shook her head, not wanting to relive those horrifying moments again. She lathered her hair and inhaled peace as much as scent. She couldn't help but be reminded of the place she'd come from. The dead animal smells of the forest-encased farmland surrounding what she'd always considered home came to mind, but she pushed them away, too. She hadn't been told, until just as Sara was helping her to escape, those smells were because massive numbers of animals were being experimented on and killed, just liked they wanted to do with her. Sara said the land was nothing more than a graveyard. And after she explained what one was, Isabella decided she'd wished she hadn't asked.

That place had never been her home, and those people hadn't been family. At least Sara cared enough to send Isabella away when her life was at risk, but even *she* had allowed them to poke at her and pick her brain for those years.

Isabella just hoped Sara hadn't paid too large a price for finally letting her go.

Now knowing the man she'd only known as *Doc* all her life, was willing to kill her rather than see her free, made Isabella afraid for the woman. But there was nothing she could do about any of it, not even have someone go back to see if Sara was okay.

Isabella had no idea where *back* was... Once she'd escaped, she'd driven without any idea of where she was going either. All she'd known at the time was she had to get as far away as fast as she could. That she'd ended up here, with someone who understood her oddities better than she did herself, put her fears to rest, or at least gave her a peace she'd never expected to have again.

She hadn't been lying when she told Apollo what he did, and what he promised to do, was everything. If not for his kindness and abilities, she would be dead or *worse*, captured once again by those seeking her. She owed Apollo, and somehow she'd find a way to repay him for his kindnesses. She had no idea how yet, but she had no problem enjoying his company while she tried to figure it out.

He was a beautiful work of art, as Sara sometimes said of the men they'd secretly look over in the wrinkled old magazines Sara kept hidden away. If Apollo's features were any indication, he had the Native American Indian heritage like those she'd seen and had started to learn to read about and fantasized about meeting face to face. Were it not for Sara, and those forbidden things she shared, Isabella would never have known such men existed.

She'd coveted those few times she was allowed to look at what Sara called her stash. With men checking in at all times of the day, and inspections held regularly where they'd even look through the trash, Sara rarely ever pulled them out from the back of her closet where she kept them wrapped in an old blanket. Her friend had always been fearful they'd be found, and she would be punished. Now that she knew a bigger world existed, Isabella was afraid Sara had been as much a prisoner as she.

If the so-called doctor had his way, Isabella realized, she would have never gotten any type of an education. Thankfully, Sara made sure she did, even if it was limited to a few books, the magazines, gardening in their back yard, and driving... The sudden realization Sara had prepared Isabella to leave at some point only made her more concerned the woman was now the one in danger, causing a sick feeling in the pit of her stomach. She rode it out, letting the water wash it away, as there was nothing else to do.

Isabella rinsed her hair and then lifted the bottle of conditioner. It too had the woodsy smell and made her hair slick enough to flatten the loose curls laying over her breasts and stringing down her abdomen when the water ran through the long strands again.

She took a few minutes longer after she finished washing than she probably should have, just to enjoy standing in what felt like a hard rain. The luxury of taking her time was as new as everything else she now experienced. At the compound, before they'd let her live in the little house, her showers were limited to no more than five minutes. There was no pleasure in the frantic scrubbing down and covering herself up, before one of the men who guarded her at night barged in to tell her time was up. After the move, Sara had told her to be just as fast, as the amount of water they used was monitored just like everything else.

"Don't think about them."

Saying the words aloud held no power. Isabella knew she'd be looking over her shoulder for a long time to come. She was placing her trust in Apollo because *he* believed he could protect her, but also because there was no other choice but to do so.

Eventually she would have to find a way to take care of herself, but with the threat to her life still too large to ignore, and her lack of education and experience, she had no idea how she would. The only thing she knew, for certain, was going back to that life was not an option.

After drying off Isabella wrapped a second towel around her hair, making a turban she settled on top of her head. She dreaded what came next. The long tresses were a pain to brush through, though now they seemed so much slicker than normal since she'd gotten to use the conditioner. Of course, she didn't have a brush, so that was a problem too.

"Isabella?"

Isabella looked at the door and the feelings of someone waiting outside of it *again* sent her heart into overdrive. She wrapped herself quickly with the towel she dried off with, and clutched it to her chest. "Yes?"

"I wanted to let you know I'll have some clothes for you shortly. My cousin Sapphire will bring them over as soon as she gets back to her house and can return. Is there anything else you need right now?"

Her nerves settling again, Isabella blew out a breath. "Um… I don't want to trouble you. You've already done so much."

There was a slight pause, before Apollo responded, "Tell me what you need. No trouble, I promise."

Just ask! "I need a hair brush. Or a comb. And I need to brush my teeth."

"I'm on it!"

She couldn't help but smile at Apollo's quick, chipper, response. "Thank you," she called out, and dropped the towel on the tiled floor, wondering how she'd landed in such a wonderful place with an equally wonderful man.

It could have gone so differently, and she wasn't about to forget it. No matter what Apollo needed from her, she'd be whatever that was. She'd learn to cook for him. And clean, though it was obvious that wouldn't be a chore. His place was immaculate, but now she could help him keep it that way.

Knowing she was grasping at very small straws, Isabella worried over what value she would actually be to a man who obviously needed nothing she had to offer. He was totally fit, his muscular toned body amazing, which meant he already ate well, and the house was already perfect. What did that leave? There was no way she could stay very long if she didn't think of some way to be useful. It wasn't fair to him, and it would make her feel less than she already did.

The more she thought on it, the worse Isabella felt. She probably couldn't even carry on an intelligent conversation with the man. She knew nothing of the world. Nothing of anything, really. She sighed deeply, realizing she was nothing.

Isabella exited the bathroom after taking the time to wipe down the wet tiles, and pulling his shirt over her head, which thankfully fell to her knees. The shorts he gave her fit well enough when rolled over a few times, since his hips were slim, but the crotch of them hung nearly to her knees as well, and felt more awkward than going without. She just hoped his cousin remembered underwear, too!

In the meantime, she'd just have to be brave. And careful how she sat.

She carried her wet items to the living room to find Apollo at the front door. He looked back and smiled at her, and waved her forward.

"You'll want to see this."

Curious, she moved forward, and stopped at his side. She clutched to wet clothing to her chest as a beautiful black wolf with saddle bags strapped to its back slowly approached the house with its nose up in the air, as if sniffing for danger. She looked from it to Apollo, only to see him smiling delightedly. She turned to study the wolf again. "Is it your pet?"

"She's my cousin."

No sooner had he said the words the wolf shook the pack from her back where it landed at her side. Only a second passed from leather hitting the ground before the wolf shook her head and her body transformed into that of a dark-haired, beautiful, *naked* woman. The gasp that passed Isabella's lips was more awe than anything else, but the reality of what she'd just witnessed knocked her senses, and she stumbled toward Apollo.

Apollo caught her quickly and held her securely, and Isabella found herself captured by the amusement in his blue eyes. Her nipples hardened, her body hummed, and she was certain the air touching her upper thighs indicated his shirt had bunched up, and no longer lay over what it was meant to cover. Were she not so spellbound, she would have let the fact that, were it not for Sara, she would still think nothing of men seeing her nude.

The amusement lighting Apollo's eyes changed to something else as he stared at her, and whatever was making him look at her in that way stole the breath from her lungs. He set her away from him gently but continued to stare, as if he couldn't bear to break contact. Only the sound of the door's handle clicking pulled her from this trance. She blinked several times in an attempt to clear her muddled mind before she realized the woman, *now completely clothed*, was opening the screened door.

The most amazing blue eyes Isabella had ever seen stared back at her curiously, until finally, his cousin turned her attention to Apollo.

"You allowed her to see?"

There was no anger in the woman's voice, but caution was clearly there. Isabella licked her lip and raised her hands before Apollo could answer, and before she lost her nerve. She closed her eyes and thought of the items in the room, lifting each one, after the other, and slowly spun them around at her back. She envisioned returning each to its original spot, and sighed as she opened her eyes. Apollo must have turned around at some point to watch the show, and was now facing her with astonishment. His cousin stepped in the door, her eyes twinkling, her lush lips lifted in a smile.

"Well, that was interesting."

Isabella nodded. "Not nearly as much as what you did."

"The eye of the beholder. I'm Sapphire, by the way."

"I'm Isabella. It's nice to meet you. And thank you for bringing me some things. As you must have seen. I have little."

One of Sapphire's brows rose high. "From what I saw, you have something special. But since you're talking about your girl parts being exposed, don't give it a thought. Nudity for us girls around here is only relevant if there is a special man involved."

With a saucy grin at Apollo, Sapphire walked past them to place the packs on the couch. "I brought you a couple pairs of jeans and a few shirts, underwear and a bra." She turned back and looked Isabella over. "I would have brought more if I was certain of your size, but I think these will do just fine for now."

Gratitude seemed to be the word of the day. Isabella moved toward Sapphire as she pulled the items out of the packs. "Thank you, so much. I don't know if Apollo told you, but I'm in a bit of trouble."

Sapphire reached out and took her hands. "All he told me was you were here, needed protection from people hunting you, and that you had nothing, and could I help out. He left out the part that you are a mystic of some kind. But it's nice to find someone outside of the family who is. That's very rare."

Isabella had always felt her differences a burden to despise. To see they meant something to someone who bore her no ill will was too new to process. She nodded as Sapphire released her, before turning back to find Apollo staring at them both from the front door. His smile came slowly, before he looked to his cousin.

"Thank you for bringing those."

She nodded. "I'll bring more, and anything else needed." She glanced to Isabella. "Anything."

"Thank you. I know that's so little to say because all this means so much. But thank you!"

Sapphire nodded, searching Isabella's eyes. "You are more than welcome. If you'd like, I can bring some magazines here, and you can show me what styles you like. I'll order what you need on the Internet from my house, since *he who doesn't like to be on anyone's radar* doesn't own a computer, and have it sent to my house." She grinned. "Apollo has no actual address either, anyway, as far as the postal service knows. In your case this is a good thing, since there will be no evidence of a woman's clothing coming directly here, to him, and possibly leading someone to you."

"I hadn't thought of that. Thanks, cuz," Apollo said, watching them both.

Sapphire approached him, her slender, jean-encased hips reaffirming to Isabella they were about the same size, if you discounted Sapphire's longer legs. The relief these two people were the ones to protect her brought tears to

Isabella's eyes. The reality that she really was safe, possibly for the first time in her life, nearly collapsed her knees. She stood firm and watched as the cousins kissed each other's cheeks.

"The family should know everything."

Apollo looked over his cousin's shoulder and winked at Isabella as he spoke to her. "I know. And they will have to. But for now, let's give Isabella time to adjust." He grinned and pulled back. "Everyone wanting to visit at once will be a little overwhelming."

Isabella moved toward them. "Are you all...*special?*"

Sapphire turned to face her and nodded. "In one way or another. We call what we have and can do *gifts* and have come to think of ourselves, en masse, as mystics. There is none among us who would bring you harm. We too must guard who and what we are."

Isabella nodded, knowing they were placing as great a trust in her as she was in them. "I would like to meet everyone, if my doing so doesn't bring this danger to you all."

Sapphire and Apollo smiled almost identical smiles.

"You don't have to worry about that," he said. "My family has centuries of learning how to take care of their own."

"Can I tell everyone what I know?" Sapphire asked.

The simple fact of being asked, rather than told what was going to happen in her life was another first. Isabella nodded. "Please do. And tell them I look forward to meeting them, as well."

Sapphire kissed Apollo's cheek again before she walked out the door. Isabella hurried to Apollo's side and marveled as Sapphire shed her clothing with a swipe of her hand, before she was again the little wolf. The beautiful animal turned her head back to face them, and Isabella was certain the wolf actually smiled. She watched it take off at a lope before picking up speed and disappearing into the tree line.

"She's amazing."

Apollo nodded. "Yes she is. But so are you. How did you do what you did?"

Isabella shrugged. "I don't know. I just think about moving things, and they go there." She bit her lip, knowing he deserved to know the rest. "I can do other things too with my mind. But I've never let anyone else know. I realized when I was very young that something was off about the people who wanted me to believe they were my family. For years, they just fed me and clothed me and asked me to make things move. I tried to hug them in the early years when I thought I'd pleased them." The memory made her frown. "I guess it's natural to want human contact and affection even if you've never had it, but they just pushed me away. They finally brought in a woman, Sara, a couple of years ago. She gave me hugs and much warmer attention than the men never had. She taught me things rather than just expecting me to perform, but even her options were limited under their watchful eyes.

"I knew they paid her to be with me, and I eventually figured out they meant for the closeness between us to help them get me to cooperate when I recently started becoming defiant. When she learned they were going to kill me, to dissect my brain and body to see what was different about it, she helped me to escape. I fear she has paid dearly for it."

****

Apollo felt the air leave his lungs. He'd known there were threats to his family, by being discovered, but he'd never imagined there were people in the world who would go to such horrific lengths to understand why some people were extraordinarily gifted and some not.

He held his arms open and fought letting the warmth

of her body against his mean anything more than comfort given and accepted. His attraction to her was acceptable, as she was an incredibly beautiful young woman. But she was also innocent in so many ways. He held her loosely for the second time, not wanting her to know how much she touched him, both physically and emotionally.

When Isabella stepped back and looked up, he waited heartbeats, certain she didn't realized there was desire in her spinning deep green eyes. He licked his lips, instinctually, and then looked above her head to the room at large. If he continued to stare at her, he was afraid he'd kiss her, until one of them, or possibly both, went blind.

Chapter Three

Sara Richardson cried out again before lifting a hand to her bloodied lips. She'd known letting Izzy go free would cost her a job, but she never expected to be beaten to death. She tilted her head so she could look through the one eye still working, trying to gauge where her tormentor was. The other eye was swollen shut, but she feared blindness wasn't going to be a problem once they were through with her.

"I'm sorry," she said hoarsely, knowing the loss of her voice was because of the hand that squeezed her throat only seconds before the large fist smashed her lips. They wanted her to give them information since they'd lost Izzy, but they weren't making it easy for her to do. They wanted to know what she'd taught Izzy besides driving, as well, such as who Sara sent their lost prisoner to for help.

Sara was glad her former charge had gotten away, but now had to worry about herself. As much as she'd come to care about the girl, Sara really didn't want to die in her place. "I'll tell you everything I know!" she screamed only seconds before the next fist landed.

Sara's head hit the floor hard, and still she didn't black out. At this point, she knew several bones in her face had to be broken, and knew too, they'd probably decided she wouldn't be helpful anyway and were just going to go on and kill her.

Pain slammed through every part of her as they sat her chair back up and dragged her onto it. She wobbled and nearly fell out again, but large hands crushed already agonized shoulders to hold her in place.

"Clean her up and lay her down. I'll be back in a few hours to see what she has to say."

Sara tried not to scream out as her arms were gasped at the armpits and her ankles as well, but her entire body was a writhing mass of agony, and she couldn't help herself.

"*Now*, she wants to get vocal."

The laughter of the two men didn't touch Sara. She'd always known them to be rude. The brutes were hired long before she was, to make sure Izzy remained in custody and to make sure Sara never did anything to help the girl discover what a pitiful life she'd always lived. They had to enjoy seeing that she was the one being punished, rather than them.

They tossed her onto the bed Izzy once used, and she rolled on her side and curled up as much as her pain-filled ribs would allow. She ignored their taunts, their joking, and let the tears fall.

Chapter Four

Nervous energy sat like a third passenger between her and Apollo, as his truck turned into the driveway of his parents' home. Her confidence when she'd spoken to Sapphire the day before about meeting the entire family was sincere. Now the moment had actually arrived to do so, and she was terrified.

What if someone didn't like her? What if her presence posed too great a risk for each of the family members to ignore? What would she do if some of them insisted Apollo set her loose to fend for herself, so she couldn't bring danger to their doors?

The questions ate at her until she turned to him abruptly. "Maybe we shouldn't do this!"

Apollo stopped the truck immediately and pushed it into park. He turned to her, his gaze filled with compassion, not the anger she feared would be there.

"If you aren't ready, we'll go back to our place."

She didn't know which to grasp first, that he'd abort what was already set in motion on her behalf, or that he'd included her when speaking of his home. Sara took a deep breath and smiled. "Is everyone in the outside world as nice as you?"

Looking almost abashed, Apollo shook his head.

"There are a lot of good people in the world, and still too many who aren't. Usually, growing up, you develop a radar for such things, but there are those who will still surprise you in the end."

Sara nodded slowly, knowing she had learned those things too late. She was afraid her experience was too limited, still, for her to be able to make the distinction when it came to meeting someone new.

"Your family… They are all good people?"

Apollo's features relaxed, giving her the answer before he spoke.

"We believe we are only what we are because we are meant to do good deeds regarding both the earth and mankind."

"And still you live in fear?"

Apollo hesitated only a second. "Not in fear, but with caution."

She digested that, her curiosity growing. "Sapphire. For what purpose is there such a being?"

Apollo turned off the truck and settled back against the seat. "Sapphire had the ability to wield magic before she became a Lycanthrope, but she never used it because she feared it had harmed someone when she was young. She learned later she was wrong about that, and now she uses it when she needs to, to help any who may need her help in that way. But she often relies on the more human way of doing things in her position of a police officer for Mystic Waters. She only became a Lycanthrope after she met the man she married. And even in that form, as you saw, she was happy to come to our aid."

Apollo's brows drew together. "In the local pack of Lycanthrope, Sapphire is the Alpha Female. That means she holds high status and is only second to the Alpha Male when it comes to leading the pack. She, and *they*, make up the security system I alluded to yesterday morning. Several are even now patrolling the mountain, guarding us. They have been since I first spoke to Sapphire about you."

Isabella was stunned at the generosity of those Apollo knew, but she had no idea what a Lycanthrope was and told him so.

"A werewolf."

The confusion in her eyes must have been reflected for him to see.

"A misunderstood creature who is both wolf and man or woman. When we first met her husband and his pack, they were in grave danger as well."

"So they protect you as payment for helping them?"

Apollo shook his head. "We protect each other's existence. They are our friends, and we are theirs."

Heaving a heavy sigh, Isabella looked out the windshield. "Will I get to meet more of them?"

Apollo was smiling when she turned back his way.

"You will meet at least one more today. Sapphire's husband, Nicolae. I will see you meet the others patrolling and guarding you as well. You need have no fear of them."

Relaxing back into the seat, Isabella looked ahead. "I am ready now."

Apollo restarted the truck, and they rolled forward slowly. Isabella couldn't help but look out her window, as she hoped to see more of those intriguing creatures guarding them beyond the thick stand of trees. She was a little disappointed when the tree line ended, and a grassy field replaced it, until she looked forward again.

The large log structure sitting so majestically, yet seeming to fit in perfectly with its rugged surroundings, had a large front yard filled with a multitude of people. She looked from one to another, realizing all seemed delighted to be where they were and whom they were with. Lovely women's lips lifted in smiles while they turned from one to another in what was obviously deep conversation. Though they seemed tuned in to each other, no hands stood idle, as all were busily setting up the tables for todays shared meal.

There were several men too, coming one after another from the back of the house with large chairs in their hands.

After seeing they were arranging them for a mass visitation, Isabella looked toward the tree line again, and delight filled her. Smoke rose from two large smoking devices she knew to be grills.

The relief at finding something familiar in this land of the unknown shouldn't have flooded her with as much peace as it did, but she would take what comfort she could. Although she was prepared to put on a brave face for Apollo, meeting so many strangers at once was making her shake inside the closer they got.

Knowing how silly it was to grasp onto something as simple as a cooker for reassurance, Isabella kept her thoughts to herself. But Sara grilled often….

Or she had.

Isabella refused to think about all she'd left behind. At least for now. Today wasn't about the past.

"My family finds any reason they can to throw a picnic."

Isabella turned to him with a smile, knowing her lips shook. "I didn't realize there were *that* many! Just how big is your family?"

Apollo laughed. "Just about too big to count anymore. But once you meet them, you'll think you've known them forever. They are a nosy bunch, who like to share their lives and will be more than happy to delve into yours. It's the way we were taught by our mothers to love each other. If they make you uncomfortable, at any time, just tell them to mind their own business."

Isabella turned to him. "I could never be so rude!"

His smile was lopsided and endearing.

"It won't be taken that way. We tell each other to butt out all the time. It will just make you a part of the family."

She unlatched her seatbelt, knowing everyone had stopped in the middle of what they were doing to look her way. Determined to be as brave as she could, she opened her door but had to stop when Apollo was already there. Still amazed by his speed, she took the hand he held out and was relieved he didn't let her go as they approached the mass of people gathering close together. Apollo stopped her before the older couple who stood before the others. There was no doubt in her mind she was about to meet his parents.

"Mom, Dad, this is Isabella Quinn. Isabella, these are my parents, Destiny and Tom Whitehawk.

Before she could offer a greeting, she was in the arms of the beautiful redheaded woman, being hugged *very* tightly. When Destiny released her and stepped back, there was, amazingly, joy in her greeting.

"We are so happy to meet you! Do you go by Isabella, or do you have a nickname?"

The realization everyone, including her husband, was looking at Destiny as if she'd lost her mind for giving such an enthusiastic greeting made Isabella as curious about these reactions as she was about being so quickly accepted by the woman before her. "Call me Isabella. Where I came from they always called me Izzy, so I it's a name I never want to hear again."

Destiny nodded. "Then Isabella it is." She turned to her husband. "Are you just going to stand there?"

Tom tore his gaze from his wife, and it changed from quizzical to engaging.

"Welcome to our home, Isabella. Please, make yourself comfortable."

She loved the deep sound and the cadence of Tom's voice. There was such peace in it, she couldn't help but relax. "Thank you."

Apollo swung her hand, bring her attention to him.

"Now, the rest of the gang."

Isabella smiled up at him, not an ounce of fear remaining. "Good!"

He laughed. "That's what you say now." He walked her to the far right of those gathered and began:

"This is my cousin, Jewell, who is Sapphire's next youngest sister by minutes. And this is her husband, Amenra. She can transport through time if she so desires. Which is how she met him. He came from ancient Egypt, was once a palace guard and minor prince, but now is the father to Jewell's four children, all of whom were born within minutes of each other.

She greet them, trying to process the information quickly since Apollo was already standing in front of a beautiful blond and the man whose large hand rested on her huge round belly.

"This is Diamond, who we call Dia, and her husband Ryan. Dia has power over the earth and is capable of making things grow or die, and Ryan wields his own form of magic, of the completely human variety. He builds game systems and games and is so smart he makes the rest of us look lame."

Ryan laughed at that as he extended his hand. "It's nice to meet you, Isabella. Don't let this guy fool you. He can kick butt when it comes to quick thinking and reflexes."

She smiled. "Nice to meet you too. And yes, I've seen his quickness."

Isabella turned to Dia, glad Sara had shown her a woman with a similar bump in one of her magazines. "Congratulations on the baby."

"Babies. I'm carrying three."

Although the thought of bearing three children was stunning, and a little terrifying to think about, Dia seemed perfectly content with the idea, so Isabella smiled back. "Wow. That's amazing."

"Not in our family. It's pretty much the norm." Dia looked her up and down, and her smile bloomed. "You are very young."

Isabella hadn't ever thought of her age in any context, so she didn't know how to respond, other than with facts. "I'm nearly twenty."

There was a sharp bark of coughing coming from the next man in line, which Isabella thought might have started as a laugh. She looked at him and realized, other than having additional bulk and a very different haircut, he looked exactly like Apollo. The woman at his side was gorgeous, with long black hair and penetrating eyes.

"This is my brother Zeus and, next to him his lady Sabia Ilie. They fight demons together with fire from within their bodies, and she is also Lycanthrope."

Isabella exchanged greeting with each, though she had a moment of unease when Sabia emitted a low growl when Isabella shook Zeus's hand.

"Down, girl," was Zeus's laughing comment, making everyone around them laugh as well.

"I'm sorry," Sabia said with sincerity. "Don't look frightened. It was instinctual reaction, nothing more."

Isabella nodded, pretending she understood, as Apollo moved them to the next couple. At first, she thought his mother had joined the line-up, until she realized there was a third who looked exactly like Destiny Whitehawk on the other side of the man holding this one's hand.

"This is Uncle Logan and Aunt Haven. They are the Hansens. She is of nature. Thus she has power to not only control elements on the earth but the sky as well, and she is one of three identical triplets with my mother and Aunt Rayne. Uncle Logan is a heart surgeon and tries to stay clear of her magic whenever he can."

After another round of laughter, she was being greeted warmly by his aunt and then his uncle, before she was scooted on down again.

"This is Aunt Rayne and her husband, Uncle Garrison. The Whites. Appropriately enough, she is a *white* witch and has too many powers to list, and he is a magician when it comes to building and designing everything from furniture to homes. Like my house, my parents' home is only one of his creations, as well as all the furniture within. And without, for that matter."

Isabella looked up at the large log structure beyond the crowd. As she'd already noticed, it looked at home in its setting, as if having grown from the ground beneath it. *Wow* was too impotent a response. "The house is beautiful!"

Garrison smiled at her, but then everyone did.

"Thank you, Isabella. Welcome," Garrison White said, shaking her hand respectfully.

She was stopped next in front a beautiful brunette whose soulful eyes looked back at her. The smile from this one wasn't as warm, but more cautious. Before Apollo could make the introductions, the woman did herself.

"I'm Soleli Hansen. I'm one of a set of three as well. But I have no powers."

Although she didn't look away to the others, Isabella felt the sudden tension and knew they were no longer smiling. She held out her hands, and belatedly, Soleli reached out as well. When they clasped, Isabella inhaled deeply at the unexpected vision. "You have power. It is thrumming within you and will be released when the time is right."

There were no sounds. Not even those of the birds that previously sang to each other. Until that moment, Isabella hadn't noticed them, but their sudden silence was deafening.

Soleli stared at her, the woman's deep blue eyes filled with questions and denial.

"How would you know this?"

Isabella wanted to take her words back. But now that they were spoken, she forced herself to relax. She was among friends, and these people would not harm her. Nor would they use her. They had powers of their own.

"I sometimes see into the future."

Hope sprang into Soleli's eyes. "You see my future?"

Isabella shook her head. "Not clearly. And not everything is set in stone. One decision can change it, altering the rest, but I saw you have an awakening." She frowned and shook her head. "An awakening of magic." She turned and looked up to Apollo, but he only nodded, questions in his gaze as well.

"It's hard to explain. I don't really understand it myself. It isn't something I could allow to develop because others would have wanted more from me than they were already taking. I had to keep it to myself. Suppress it. Deny it."

Apollo squeezed her hand, once again turning her attention to him. "You are free to develop it here if you choose. But the choice is yours. We help each other, but we do not use each other."

His assurance compounded what Isabella was already coming to understand. She turned back to Soleli. "If I learn of anything that will aid you, I will share it with you."

Soleli nodded and stepped forward to wrap Isabella in a hug. "You have already done so much. I just can't begin to tell you how much!"

She stepped back, tears in those dark blue eyes. "Please, forgive me," she whispered, before turning and fleeing toward the house.

Haven and Rayne went after her, and Isabella bit her lip, hoping she hadn't done something to bring pain.

"Those are tears of joy, Isabella. She's fine."

Realizing Destiny Whitehawk was at her side, she nodded. "I hope so."

The woman's smile was gentle. "I *know* so."

Isabella nodded and looked to the next person when Destiny stepped back. Apollo took up his introductions again. "This is Luna and her husband Zebulon Titanium. He is a merman, and she a mermaid. She also has the ability to heal the earth but only within the magical waters of Mystic Lake. She has other powers, too, but they are all related directly to the lake."

The auburn-haired beauty looked her over and grinned. "Welcome to our world, Isabella. It's almost like an amusement park filled with weird rides."

Her husband laughed at her joke, as did everyone standing around.

"Thank you. I think it's amazing! I think you are *all* amazing!"

"As are you."

This came from the next woman, a white-haired woman whose beauty seemed too perfect to be real. "Thank you."

"No need. It is what it is, as they say. I'm Celestia, and this dark hunk of man at my side is my Sabian. He gave up Heaven, to join with me here on earth."

The dark-haired man seemed pleased, which meant something, Isabella was sure, but all the questions building up within her would have to wait until she and Apollo were alone. Right now, she just wanted to get to know this wonderful, *amazing* family.

The last in line was another of Apollo's brothers, there was no doubt about that. But this one was thinner, though still very toned, and his features, though not feminine, were softer in some way. She wasn't certain, but she didn't think the perfectly shaped eyebrows were completely natural.

"I'm Heracles."

Isabella returned the greeting and smiled. "It's nice to meet you."

"You as well."

Since no one was sharing his magical ability, she didn't ask. And she didn't reach out to him either. There were enough things for her to think about already, one of which was the amazing smells coming from the black grills. When she mentioned it, Apollo's brothers barked out an identical curse before they immediately ran to the cookers. Not as quickly as Apollo would have, she was sure.

"If they burned the ribs, I'm going to kick their butts," Apollo said with a laugh.

Everyone laughed with him, as Sapphire approached. "Would you like to come with me and help in the kitchen? Apollo can go over there and make sure his brothers don't ruin our meal."

Chapter Five

Her body was one big mass of anguish, her sight nearly completely gone.

Sara would give anything to be able to go back in time, but unlike those souls these people kept caged like animals, she had no special abilities. She wouldn't have taken the job as caretaker for the woman-child The Barnabas Group hired her for, even though the pay was so outrageous. She hadn't known in the beginning what they were, or what they did, and after learning, she'd been too afraid to attempt leaving.

She'd only been here a short time before realizing those being caged were extraordinary in some way. It was much later before she learned of Maximum Barnabas and the lengths he was willing to go to find what he called creatures of darkness.

"I see you are awake."

Dread was a physical manifestation as it ringed fire down her body from head to her toes. She waited for them to lift her and return her to the chair of torture, but instead saw movement as she looked up. With only one good eye left, and it not so good, she couldn't make out the face of the man standing over her.

"I will tell you all I can. Just, please, let me go. I'll never breathe a word about any of this!"

Chapter Six

Leaving Apollo's side was hard to do.

Isabella had never felt such security as she did with him, but knew it was time to start taking care of herself, even if in this small way. She walked between Sapphire and Destiny, accepting the smiles from those now returning to whatever chore or play they'd been at before she and Apollo arrived.

The few stairs leading up to the wide front porch were lacquered, cut from trees split in half, and turned so the flatter side was up. There was wear on the steps, but they were still as slick as the wide porch itself. It spanned the entire front of the house, and then it went around on the side facing a large open field. Trees, with the curious eyes of small animals peeking out, were close to the house on the other side, as if the forest only stopped in deference to those humans who had made this their home.

Large wooden porch chairs and tables looked as if they'd sprouted from the earth as well. Her marveling didn't stop as she entered a screened front door and arrived in what was clearly the living room. Though finer in design, the furniture here was also made of wood, but thick leafy-printed cushions made them look like comfortable places to sit and relax.

She bypassed them as she followed the women across the large room to where Soleli and the two other matriarchs were already pulling items from the refrigerator and large oven, to place them on the surface of the long island that separated the kitchen from the living room. The bowls filled with a vast variety of foods were huge, but that made sense given the size of the family gathered.

The smiles that came her way instantly warmed her, and Isabella knew a peace of place as never before. "What can I do to help?"

"Anything you want. We need to get these dishes outside to the tables, but do you mind if we get to know each other a little more first?"

Asked, not demanded. What a refreshing change, Isabella though, knowing they had as many questions as she. "What would you like to know?"

The three women looked at each other, then to her, but Soleli was the first to speak. "You're so young. How did you manage to get away from the people Sapphire told us about?"

Since she'd expected Soleli to ask something about herself, her *future*, as it had seemed so important just moments before, it took a moment to switch gears.

Isabella thought back to the compound, and all it represented, and pressed her lips together. She no longer felt fear. That had been replaced with overwhelming anger. With determination, she repressed the fire stirring in her gut. She didn't want it to be a part of today. Or any days to follow, if she could help it. The sooner she could put her past behind her, the sooner her life would really be her own. But first, she owed them all as much of an explanation as she could give.

"I don't know too much about the place I came from, although I learned more as the woman who helped me escape took me through the building where the experiments were conducted. But from that point on, things only got more confusing.

"Sara, my only real friend, taught me to drive some time ago, although my experience isn't great. When she realized how much danger I was really in, she took me to the gates of the compound. Up until then, they were the end of the world as far as I knew it. She told me to take the car and go to the left onto the road, to keep driving until I reached a place to hide. It was the only way I'd ever be safe.

"It felt like I drove forever. When I saw the mountains, it felt right to turn and go up one. It wasn't until I was descending on the other side that I knew she was wrong in thinking I'd be free of them. They must have been following at a distance all along.

"With so little experience, and I guess because I was afraid, too, I never looked back, and I drove slower than everyone else on the road. If the men following me hadn't been behind me the whole time, they could have easily caught up to me after a while.

"With Apollo's help I got away from them, after they tried to kill me on the mountain road, but now I'm afraid they'll come back here, and that endangers you all."

There was silence when she finished, until Destiny reached over and took her hand. "What kind of experiments, and why do you think they can bring harm to us as well?"

Isabella looked into the eyes of her savior's mother, amazed she was old enough to have grown sons. "They experimented on children to try to learn why they had...*unusual* abilities. If it weren't for the impending ending of my life, so they could dissect me, Sara would never have been brave enough to help me escape."

Thinking of the woman nearly made Isabella ill, and that only increased her fear. If Sara was now in danger, it was all Isabella's fault.

"That's horrible!"

Nodding to Soleli who looked back in horror, Isabella sighed.

"There are more like you? Like us? And you say they are children?" Destiny asked, her face pale.

Isabella nodded. "Yes. Only a few I think. I never knew they were there until that last day. I only saw them as Sara rushed me out of the building. There's a line of rooms with large glass windows. I didn't think about it then, but now realize I'd been moved through each of those rooms as I got older. The first is basically a nursery, then one with toddler toys I played with when I was very young, and then the last, the one I've been tested in since I turned thirteen, is filled with things I guess were to interest me at my age."

Isabella blew out a breath. "I think Sara is the one who told them what those things should be once she came into my life."

"This *Sara* person, where is she now?"

The controlled anger in Rayne's voice pulled Isabella's attention her way.

"I don't know. I hope she got away, but I had the car, and there isn't a town for many miles. I fear what they will do to her, if she was caught."

"Why didn't she leave with you?"

Isabella shrugged. "I don't know. Everything happened so fast, I never thought to ask her."

"You can't blame yourself."

Isabella looked to Destiny. "She saved me. I should have thought about her."

"You are a baby. She is the adult. She should have come with you, if for no other reason than to make sure you got away safely."

Isabella didn't take insult at being referred to as a baby, since she knew she was in so many ways. And she couldn't give herself the out Destiny was offering either, but she knew there was no point in saying so.

"You guys going to bring that food out or what?"

They all turned, as if one, to find Heracles standing there with irritation in his eyes, one of which looked very red and possibly on the road to swelling.

"Have you boys been fighting again? Today? *Really?*" Destiny advanced on Heracles, snagged his arm, and dragged him back though the living room and out the front door, letting it bang closed behind them.

Isabella didn't move, until Rayne and Soleli began laughing. She looked at each one in turn, her own lips indecisive, as whether or not to join in. She looked to Rayne as the oldest. "Someone's been fighting with Heracles?"

Rayne's smile got even bigger. "He and his brother. That's how they play. You'd think they would have grown out of it by now. But they enjoy it too much."

Having never heard of such a concept, Isabella frowned. "It looks like Destiny is mad."

Soleli moved closer. "Oh, she'll go out there and rip them all a new one, and then set up their next boxing match I imagine." She grinned. "How do you think they learned to fight? It sure wasn't Uncle Tom. He's the most peaceful of souls there is, and he's the only thing keeping Aunt Destiny from turning to the dark side completely."

Rayne's laughter held reproach, but it was clear to see Soleli's assessment of Apollo's mother would go unchallenged. Since she'd yet to see that side of the woman, there was nothing she could say about that either, but she couldn't help but ask, "Rip them a new what?"

****

Eating and listening took up the next couple of hours. Isabella was lost in the number of conversations, the teasing that went on between the family members, and the general chaos that made up this intriguing group of people. Apollo hadn't left her side since the food was displayed, piled on plates, and they settled next to each other in two of the many chair circling the front yard.

She offered little other than when a question or comment came her way, but not out of shyness or discomfort. It was a pleasure to feel a part of a family, to watch how they interacted, and to see the affection they felt for each other held no bounds.

"Let me take your plate."

Apollo stood, so Isabella started to rise as well. "I can take it."

He waved her back down. "No problem. I'm heading to take mine in anyway. Is there anything else you want first?"

The thought of eating another bite was impossible. She relaxed back into the seat and shook her head. "Do you all eat like this all the time?"

"Individually, no. But we get together as often as possible." His brows pulled together. "Unfortunately, now that everyone has their own lives, and Zeus and Heracles are gone from home most of the time, it isn't often enough anymore."

She nodded as he walked off with the plates and then grinned when Luna dashed over to take his seat.

"Hi!"

"Hi," she returned, looking the mermaid over, wondering if she'd ever get to see the fish tail like the one in the children's book. Now that she thought about it, Isabella realized she looked a lot like the little red-haired cartoon character and, more than any of the other female cousins, looked most like the three mothers.

"Are you having a good time?"

Isabella nodded. "The best of my entire life."

Luna nodded. "I know, right? Being around my family is so much fun. Do you play sports? That's what always follows these meals. It's everyone's way of working off the gluttony."

Too embarrassed to admit her lack of education, she didn't ask what gluttony was, but she could only assume it meant consuming so much food. "I don't know sports," she said, deciding she had no choice there. If they wanted her to participate in something, she'd rather everyone know up front she was out of her element.

"Oh, you don't have to worry about it. The boys will let their food settle while we all ride around on four-wheelers, and then they'll probably move on to golf. Which I have no interest in whatsoever, although now that Zeb has learned how to play, he loves it. Then when we've all digested for a while, touch football." She grinned again. "We girls can play or not. So don't feel like you have to if you don't want to."

Before she could process all of that, Luna looked around quickly and then back as fast. "I don't mean to pry, but did you really see my sister getting her magic?"

The abrupt change in subject threw her, but Isabella was getting used to the fast and furious pace of conversation from Luna at this point. She nodded. "I did."

"But you don't know when or why?"

Isabella took a moment to think about the quick flash of vision touching Soleli brought. She shook her head. "No. It seems she was someplace dark, but I don't remember anything more than that."

Luna nodded, as if in thought, before her wide smile returned. "Well, it's something. I'm afraid she has been worried sick she would be the only one of us without a gift. The rest of us have too, but only because we know it means so much to her."

"You are all so close."

"We are. Having each other is the greatest gift any of us possess."

Since she'd never had anyone, Isabella could only agree.

Apollo made his way to them, looking from Luna to her.

"What's up, Fish-Cuz?"

Luna rolled her eyes heavenward. "Funny. *No!* I'm not asking about your prowess, if that's what you're worried about, although I question it, *Speed-O*. I was just getting to know Isabella a little better. But I'm off. Zeb will be looking for me!" She reached over and grabbed Isabella's hand and squeezed. "I'm so happy you are here."

Isabella nodded, but Luna was up and jogging across the yard before she could respond in kind. She looked up to find Apollo frowning down at her. "What is it?"

His lips tilted at an odd angle, and he shrugged. "I hope that didn't bother you."

"Luna?"

He nodded. "Yes."

"What did she do that might have bothered me?"

One beat and then another passed before he answered. "Talking about my prowess."

"What is your prowess?"

Apollo took his seat and settled back before pinning her with his gaze. "What do you know about…men and women?"

Isabella took a moment and thought about it. "Not much I guess. Before I met you all, the men in my life have only been interested in my mind control, and the only woman I've ever known was Sara."

He sat forward and grasped his hands, resting them on his knees. "That's all?"

She nodded, having no idea where this was leading, but could tell he was uncomfortable with her limited knowledge. Isabella felt self-conscious as a result. "Is that a problem?"

Apollo shook his head and looked across the yard to where several of the women had gathered as they started cleaning off the buffet. She wasn't sure he was being entirely honest, which made her feel even worse. "Please don't do that."

He glanced her way. "Do what?"

"Lie to me. People have done it my whole life. I need to know you won't."

His eyes reflected his discomfort. "I'm sorry. I shouldn't have. But I don't really know what to say."

Ready to hear something horrible about herself, Isabella pushed on. "Tell me what you are really thinking, even if you are afraid it will hurt my feelings."

A small smile lifted his lips. "I'm thinking I'd like to kiss you." And then he bit his bottom lip before adding, "But I don't think I should."

Unusual feelings stirred within her, but since she didn't know what they meant, or how to respond, Isabella looked away.

"That's why I didn't say anything. I knew it would make you uncomfortable."

She exhaled a shaky breath. "Why would you want to?"

Sapphire suddenly appeared before them, and she sent Apollo a sympathetic glance before holding a hand out to Isabella.

"Come with me, it's girl time!"

As she pulled Isabella to her feet, Apollo also stood. "Where are you taking her?"

Isabella turned his way, curious by the odd tone of his voice. But Sapphire seemed not to notice, or else she didn't care.

"Don't you worry, cuz. She'll come back to you in the original packaging," she smirked. "Only more up to speed."

A look passed between them Isabella couldn't decipher, but there was no anger it seemed, so she let it pass.

"I think I can handle it on my own," he offered, thoughtfully.

Sapphire's gentle grin seemed almost sympathetic.

"I'm sure you can, but some things girls should learn

from other girls."

"You aren't supposed to be listening with those werewolf ears of yours unless invited."

"I didn't, but Sabia unapologetically did," Sapphire said with a laugh. "So we agreed an intervention was in order."

"We, as in you and Sabia?" Apollo asked.

"We, as in all of us with vaginas."

Isabella had had enough of being left out of a conversation that was clearly about her. "Why would everyone with a vagina want to talk to me?"

Since Isabella directed the question to Sapphire, she was the one to respond. "Let's just say we are going to talk about things girlfriends share with each other, about boys."

Since she'd never been around either, as friends, it seemed like a good idea. Just learning the Whitehawk brothers liked to fight, enough to leave marks on each other, was very confusing. "Okay. I'd like to learn about boys. And girls for that matter. I've never been around them either, except one. And she wasn't a girl. She was an older woman."

Sapphire smiled. "We'll start at the beginning then. And we'll end with the birds and the bees."

"Sapphire," Apollo said with a frown, "Not too much."

As Isabella was being pulled toward the house, Sapphire threw back, "Don't worry, cuz. We'll leave the most important stuff to you…maybe."

****

Apollo fell back into the chair and rubbed his hands over his face. Isabella was nothing more than a child in a woman's body, and he was seriously concerned the women in his life were going to bombard her with too much information and frighten her for life.

He didn't want her afraid. But he didn't want her to think of him like a father or brother either. Something happened inside of him when she was near, or even looked his way from across the yard. It wasn't purely animal lust, although he had to admit that was there as well.

It was with mixed feelings that he followed their progress to the other women at the tables, as well as when all of them carried the leftovers into the house.

Heracles jogged over and settled in the chair Isabella had vacated. "She very pretty."

Apollo nodded. "Yep."

"She fits right in with everyone."

Again, "Yep."

"You like her?"

Since this was Heracles, and his attraction to women never seemed deeper than like, he nodded again. "Yep."

"Mom is over the moon about her. I've never seen her acting so nice to anyone. I think she is already planning the wedding."

Apollo frowned. "*What* wedding?"

Heracles laughed. "I'm just kidding. Sort of. It's like she's just been waiting for one of us to bring home a girl. I'm glad it's you."

The conversation was starting to get uncomfortable. "Zeus has a girl."

"*That* girl, then. As in, one who is interested in making a home for one of her boys and grandbabies for her. Zeus and Sabia are animals to each other, which is fine since it is what they both want, but *this* girl is the one Mom has been waiting for. I can feel it."

Apollo shrugged. "I think everyone is getting a little ahead of themselves."

Chuckling, Heracles agreed. "But when has that ever mattered around here?"

"This is different. Isabella isn't one of us."

There was silence for a moment before Heracles turned to face Apollo fully. "Who are you trying to convince? Me? Or yourself?"

"Don't make me black the other eye."

Heracles leaned away. "Don't! I've got a shoot in Athens in two weeks. If we were normal, I'd have to wear a steak for a week just to straighten this one up. You guys know it's anywhere but the face. *Then* you're messing with my income."

Apollo couldn't help but grin. "Sorry about that. I was aiming for your chest. You shouldn't have ducked."

"Lucky for us all, Haven can fix it. But, still. Never the face."

Apollo nodded, his gaze drifting to the front door. "Won't happen again. At least not on purpose. Bathing suits or underwear this time?"

Heracles relaxed back in the seat. "Both. Two contracts. A new company. The owner is going to be at the shoot. Which means it's going to be a pain in the ass."

"That's what happens when you pose for magazines, bro. The people paying for the ads are actually interested in the outcome."

"They usually just wait until the pictures come out, and the ad agency shows them options. This one is very hands-on, from what I understand."

Sending his brother a smirk, Apollo shook his head. "Am I to feel sorry for you? You make bank by standing around in exotic places in your panties, usually with super models hanging all over you. Forgive me if I can't find a tear to shed."

"Yeah, well," Heracles said with a deep sigh, as he stood, "it isn't always all it's cracked up to be."

Heracles no sooner made himself scarce, and Zeus plopped down. "The women are up to something."

Since Zeus sounded as annoyed about it as Apollo felt, Apollo relaxed. "Yeah. They think they need to educate Isabella on the facts of life."

Zeus frowned. "What facts?"

"Sex."

His oldest brother turned to him with amusement. "You're kidding."

Commiseration lost, Apollo felt grumpiness settling in again. "Nope."

"She's an adult."

"Barely that, and only physically. Sheltered doesn't begin to describe her life."

"So what's the deal? Are you going to claim her?"

He hadn't thought it out completely, but the need for *the claiming* was exactly what he feared was happening. It was the only reason he hadn't protested Sapphire whisking Isabella off to begin her sex education.

Which made him a selfish bastard.

"How long has it been since you got laid?"

Apollo turned to his brother, annoyed. "Seriously, dude?"

"Yeah. I'm serious. If it's been too long, and you claim her, you are probably going to disappoint her. Maybe you should find some pussy to build up your stamina and staying power first."

"I'm going to punch you."

"Just saying."

"Keep your saying to yourself. I don't like the word pussy, anyway. It's vulgar."

"That's just because *you* are a pussy."

Apollo jumped from his seat and pulled his fist back, but Zeus was up, and as ready to tangle. They stared at each other, Apollo furious, his chest heaving, and Zeus amused.

"Come on, little brother. I'm not the punk. I'll give you two black eyes to my one."

"Hey!"

They both turned at their mother's shout and dropped their hands. Apollo glanced at Zeus and was pleased to see him as repentant as Apollo was himself. "This isn't over," he said quietly.

Zeus grinned. "Damn, I sure hope not."

Chapter Seven

"You ready to talk?"

Sara tried to keep her balance as she'd been allowed to stay on the bed, as long as she could sit up on her own. "I am."

"Where did she go?"

She had no idea, but telling them the truth would probably get her killed instantly. Sara didn't believe they'd ever let her leave, or live for that matter, but if she stalled, maybe there was a chance she could escape.

"I told her to head east. To follow a certain path. I have no idea if she did."

"We know she made it to the mountains of West Virginia! We want to know who you know there that would have taken her in!"

West Virginia? The mountains? Sara tried to focus and figure out what she should say next. Apparently, she took too long, as pain slammed into her jaw and sent her sprawling back on the bed.

"Sit her up!"

Her arms screamed with the pain of being grasped with iron fists, the rest of her did too, as she was again pulled into a sitting position.

"Answer the question now!"

"The Brooks. I sent her to find the Brooks!"

"Who are they? What have you told them about us? What's the damned address?"

Time… She needed time. "Uh, I don't know their address. I know how to get to it, but I don't know it. I didn't tell them anything. I haven't talked to them in years."

"Could you find it again? What are you to them? Would they take her in?"

Sara wanted to smile to herself, but didn't dare. There were no Brooks, there was no address, but, if she was careful, she might just get to take a road trip and have a real chance at freedom. There was no way she'd get off the compound on her own.

"I *know* I can find it. I knew them when I vacationed there when I was young. They are distant cousins. And they are very nice people, so yes, I believe they would have taken her in."

Evil laughter came at her, but she couldn't turn her head to see which of the brutes was amused. "You have a week to get your head together, and then we're going to visit your nice cousins. Which is too bad for them.

"Clean her up, fix what you can. You can't take her out in public looking like that." There was a pause, then, "Scrap that. Send some of the boys back to Mystic Waters and start putting out feelers. It's going to take at least a couple of weeks before that one will be able to make the trip. If we get Izzy before then, kill Sara. If not, we'll take that traitorous bitch for a ride."

Chapter Eight

Isabella sat quietly, looking from one woman to the next. She felt like a fool in front of them all, since she was having trouble digesting all that they'd shared.

"Do you have any questions?" Destiny asked with kindness in her emerald eyes.

Only a hundred. "I...uh. Uh."

Soft laughter filled the room, and Isabella cheeks heated. She knew they weren't really laughing at her, but it felt that way, all the same. "What does it look like?"

"Get me a pen and paper," Destiny demanded, to the room at large.

There was a quick scramble as purses were gathered and dug through, before Rayne held up her hand, and both instantly appeared. Destiny smiled as Rayne handed them over. "Thanks, sis."

"No problem. This should be interesting."

Destiny nodded. "Yeah. I never thought I'd be drawing my son's penis."

"I'm more concerned that you still know what it looks like."

The droll comment from Rayne brought more laugher. This time Isabella joined in, but only because she didn't want to look as if she had no idea why the comment was so funny.

Destiny grinned as she placed the paper on the island's countertop and made quick movements with the pen. "It's only been ten years since my boys stopped running around this mountain naked as the day they were born, sister dear.

And they all, Apollo in particular, take after their father. In every, well-endowed, way."

After a resounding "*Ewww,*" from the female cousins, Destiny finished and held it out to Isabella. She took it and knew all those standing behind her were straining to see as well. She ignored them, wondering why they bothered since most had obviously seen one before, and focused on the odd shape. She looked up at Destiny. "It isn't very pretty, is it?"

Again, the laughter, and Isabella was sure she'd had enough. "It doesn't matter," she added quickly, pushing back the stool she'd been asked to sit upon when all the women converged on the kitchen. She handed the paper back to Destiny. "It isn't like I'll ever see it. There's no reason for Apollo to take off his clothes in front of me. We aren't going to do the sex. He's my protector, and I'm his…well, whatever he wants me to be. But I'm sure he wouldn't want that. You said it was best when there was love. I don't even know what that is."

The sudden silence in the room made Isabella swallow. The stunned look on Destiny's face showed disappointment as well, if she was reading the woman right. Knowing she couldn't stand to hurt these lovely women, Isabella turned abruptly, to find the same looks of caution in the eyes of all the rest. "Please, excuse me."

They nodded as one and parted so she was free to flee. But Isabella took slow measured steps, determined to exit with much more grace than she felt. Silence followed her all the way to the door, and she was relieved to see Apollo standing just in front of the porch waiting for her with a big smile on his lips.

"Would you like to take a ride on one of the four-wheelers with me?" He looked her over, when she didn't respond. His smile faltered before those lips pressing together, and he looked past her to the door. "Or would you like to leave?"

Leaving was what she wanted most, but he'd been so happy when he mentioned the four-wheeler. It didn't matter that she still had no idea what that was. If it made him happy, that's what they'd do. "The four-wheeler first. Then I think I'd like to go home."

He nodded slowly. "Are you sure?"

She relaxed. "I'm sure."

"Then that's what we'll do."

Isabella stepped forward and took the hand he offered as she made her way down the upturned split logs. The connection instantly sent peace throughout her, and she was able to give him a real smile.

"I'm in!" Heracles yelled as he raced across the yard toward them.

Apollo shook his head. "Not this time, bro. I'd like to take her solo."

Heracles stopped short and nodded. "That's cool."

"You can help me clean up the grills," Zeus stated, snagging Heracles around the neck.

"Son of a bitch!" Heracles yelped, and a tussle started, but, again, Destiny's sharp command stopped everyone in his respective tracks.

All male eyes turned her way, but hers were only for her middle son. "Be careful."

Apollo nodded slowly. "I will."

She smiled then and turned her gaze upon Isabella. "Have fun. Apollo won't let any harm come to you."

Isabella nodded and smiled, hoping everything was well between them. "Thank you, for everything."

"Thank you, sweetheart, for making this a wonderful day. I hope you both will come back and have dinner with just Tom and me tomorrow evening."

There was both question and what Isabella felt was nervousness in Destiny's gaze. Isabella looked up to Apollo and realized he was waiting for her to decide. She nodded and once again faced his mother. "I'd like that. Thank you for asking."

The relief in those green eyes was unexpected, until Isabella realized she wasn't the only one who wanted to be liked. *A friend.* Destiny wanted to be her friend! The notion was humbling. She released Apollo's hand and moved forward, until she was again standing on the porch. "May I hug you?"

Destiny's lips split into an amazing smile, as her eyes lit and sparkled.

"I'd love that."

They embraced, but it wasn't like when Sara had hugged her. Destiny's arms were strong and the hug tight. When Destiny released her, Isabella was dumbfounded to find tears had filled the older woman's eyes. She reached out and captured one off Destiny's cheek, before looking up to see the woman wiping the others away.

"Why do you cry?"

Destiny shook her head and shrugged, and she then looked out to where her son stood waiting. "Be *very* careful."

She turned to Isabella again and this time leaned forward and placed a light kiss on each one of her cheeks. Isabella lifted her hands and touched those areas, amazed at the emotion flooding her chest.

"You be careful, as well, my dear. And take good care with my son."

Although she wasn't entirely sure of Destiny's meaning, she nodded. "I will do my best."

"I know you will."

After heaving a big sigh, she once again looked to her son. "No one else will be riding today. The forest is all yours and Isabella's."

****

Apollo led Isabella around the house, knowing all eyes were on them. He ignored them but couldn't help but wonder what was going on with his mother. She never shed a tear. *Ever.* She never called anyone sweetheart. *Ever.* That she was relieved Isabella wasn't upset with her, and had waited with what he was sure was bated breath for the dinner invitation to be accepted, was out of character on so many levels. Destiny Cavanaugh-Whitehawk never cared if anyone was angry with her. She just figured if they were, *they* were in the wrong and needed an attitude adjustment.

His mom telling him to be careful hadn't had anything at all to do with riding the four-wheeler, Apollo was sure. One, he'd been riding them over the rough mountainous terrain since he could walk, and two, of the three of them, he was the only one of the brothers who hadn't ever gotten hurt doing so.

She'd been warning him to take care where Isabella was concerned, but she needn't have bothered. There was nothing he would do to hurt Isabella, *ever.* And he knew to guard his own heart just as carefully. Just because he felt the pull of the *claiming* didn't mean he had to act on it.

"Your mother is so sweet. I don't know why everyone keeps looking at her funny when she talks to me."

Apollo grinned as they approached the large garage that housed the family toys, as well as his father's tractor and its implements. "You would have to know her better to understand. She treats you differently than the rest of us."

Isabella stopped abruptly. "Why would she do that?"

Apollo hadn't thought his words would alarm, or he never would have spoken them. Or maybe he would have, he decided. Isabella wanted complete honesty, and that he could give. "I can only guess, but I think part of it is because she genuinely likes you, and maybe part of it is because she wants me to find a nice girl, which you are, to make a family with."

Isabella shook her head. "I'm not that girl."

He didn't allow her words to cut too deep. Isabella hardly knew herself as a woman, so how was she to understand and cope with things like relationships? She'd never been exposed to couples, or families, and had probably never even thought of them before meeting his.

All of that was compounded, times three, which was pretty much the norm for his family. He and Isabella barely knew each other. She was sorely uneducated about the simplest aspects of living a normal life. He was struggling with a predestined calling to mate *he* barely understood. There was no way he'd rush her into anything, nor would he let *the claiming* dictate his actions, much less his life.

"Don't worry about any of it. Let's go for a ride, and let me show you the beauty of my home."

She placed her hand on his as he reached to turn the doorknob, to open the smallest door to the garage. "Apollo?"

He looked down into her upturned face, the innocence of her eyes the only thing keeping him from taking her lips. "Yes?"

"Do you want to have the sex with me?"

Knowing he was going to kill several women in his family, he shook his head. "It's too soon to think about such things."

She sighed. "But the others seem to think it an important part of pleasing a man. I owe you my life. I wish to please you."

Dead. One after the other. Starting with Sabia, and then Sapphire. His mother a close third.

Honesty. Complete honesty. "Sex *can* be great. And very important in a relationship between a man and a woman. But not because of gratitude. Then it loses its value."

"What is its value?"

Luna would be next, then Jewell, then Soleli…or Dia. He'd off them all before he was done. "Let's go for a ride, and then we'll talk about it."

She dropped her hand and stepped back without looking at him. Apollo pushed the door open, and then hit the switch opening the first of the three large garage doors. The four-wheelers were parked nine deep and three wide. He chose the largest in the front row, since there was plenty of room for Isabella to sit comfortably behind him, leaving a space if she so chose. He was going to make the ride slow and easy, until she became more comfortable, and then, if she wanted, they'd kick things up and take as wild a ride as she could stand.

As he approached the pegboard holding all the labeled keys, Apollo wished his family would let him handle all this at his own speed, and at Isabella's. Now they'd thrown out things that were making Isabella uncomfortable and, if he were honest, him as well. He wasn't Zeus, who took what he wanted, how he wanted it, and when and where he wanted it, with little thought for the women he'd talked about, before Sabia came into his life. And he wasn't Heracles. If the tabloids were to be believed, his youngest brother had banged a beautiful woman on every continent and left many a broken heart behind. He wasn't like either of them.

Apollo knew both brothers believed him to be something of a dork when it came to women. He wasn't. He loved women. He'd love to be making love all the time. But more, he loved being in love. He didn't care what any of them thought. He was just careful. Having his heart stabbed once was enough. More importantly, Isabella had no idea what to expect.

"Apollo?"

He looked over to find Isabella running her hand along the side of the large boat his family spent many a summer on, a curious look in her eyes. "Yes?"

"It's a boat."

He nodded. "It is."

Her lips pressed together, and she frowned. "I've never seen one except in books."

All the distress his family had managed to tighten within him came unraveled. "We'll take it out on the lake soon, if you'd like."

Her childlike smile only reaffirmed his decision to take things slowly.

"I would." She looked around the large building his family called a garage. "I've never seen these other things, either. Which one is the four-wheeler?"

With the correct key in hand, he returned to the front of the garage and pointed at the one they would take. "These are."

She looked down the long row and then back at him. "You have many."

He nodded. "They belong to all of the family, but Dad is the only one who has enough room to store them all. Same with the house. For the most part, this is where we all gather."

It seemed to take her some time to pull her gaze away from the transport as she approached him. When she looked up, she searched his eyes, and he knew the easiness between them before she met his family was still too far away for her to relax. It was a mistake to introduce her to them all so soon, but the deed was done, and regret, useless.

"I will do anything you ask of me."

Apollo shook his head, afraid this was what was on her mind. "Isabella, don't. There is nothing you need to do to please me. I'm simply happy you are in my life. You are free to do as you wish. If you want something, tell me, and it's yours. If you don't want something, the same holds true. I am not your captor. You are a free woman."

He lifted the long seat and pulled two helmets out, handing one to her.

She took it as she nodded slowly, as fear in her eyes belied the acknowledgement of her freedom.

"I have nowhere else to go."

Then Celestia, and then Rayne, and finally Haven. I'm going to kill them all!

He walked around the front of the four-wheeler and took her free hand into his. Delving into her gaze, he wanted to make himself perfectly clear. "You stay as long as you like. You go if that is your desire. You, not I, nor any of my family, dictates what you do."

She swallowed, and nodded, before he continued. "Did my mother or any one of the others say anything to you that made you think you had no choice in having sex with me?"

Isabella shook her head slowly. "No. They only told me about what they called the mechanics of it all, and that it was wonderful to experience, and that it pleased the men they cared for and loved."

Relieved the women in his family hadn't completely lost their minds and done something even more stupid, Apollo relaxed and let go of the building anger. Their misguided intentions *weren't* appropriate given the circumstances, but they had been pure of intent, out of love for him. It still grated they though he needed their help, but at least he wouldn't have to kill anyone... *Not* that he ever really would have. He smiled, and Isabella, seeming to sense all was well, did too.

"Let's go for that ride and get to know each other. If there ever comes a time you want me, as a woman wants a man, then we will deal with the rest."

"Your mother says you are just like your father. That you have a kind soul. I think she is right."

Since that was the greatest complement he could ever

be given, Apollo forgave his mother her odd reactions to Isabella. "Thank you. My father is a great man."

"She said your penis was just like his too. She drew me a picture."

Cringing inwardly, Apollo counted to ten. Destiny Cavanaugh-Whitehawk and he were going to have face-time alone when he and Isabella came for dinner the following evening, because his mother had in fact lost her mind!

He pushed thoughts of his mostly wonderful but often wacky family away. He showed Isabella how to put on her helmet and mount the four-wheeler, before he climbed on. Once they settled, he started the engine and slowly drove out of the garage.

Since he wanted to see no one but the woman with him, Apollo turned abruptly to the left and took off in the direction of the pond. He was deeply aware Isabella's hands were at his sides, holding tightly at first, then more loosely as they rolled along. His natural speed could outdistance the vehicle at its highest, but he was content to troll along as they skirted a pond and approached the gate leading to a barn nearly identical to that of Logan and Haven's. Which made sense since his father and uncles had built both. Unlike his aunt and uncle, who housed the two horses Celestia rescued from a neglectful owner many months before, his parents had yet to commit to doing anything with theirs.

The evening was perfect. The breeze just enough to keep the afternoon sun from overheating their skin. He enjoyed the thrumming of power between his thighs, and the light touch of the woman at his back.

The peace of the mountain enveloped him as they rounded the barn and headed into the trees. The land instantly became rougher because of tree root, rock, and brush, and he smiled as Isabella's fingers clutched his waist harder.

There were definitely times he wondered by he hadn't acquired a more lusty persona like his brothers, but it just wasn't who he was. Like his father he felt the heartbeat of the earth, of Mother Mountain herself and knew, should he so choose, he could ask anything of her.

He hadn't, not since it cost him the woman he once believed he loved.

Not wanting to think about Scarlett, or the disaster of sharing his magic with her, Apollo increased their speed slightly, and then again. "Hold on!" he yelled turning his head to the side.

He got no response from Isabella, other than her arms wrapping around his waist when he increased the speed. Apollo let the forward momentum, the jumps over bolder-sized rocks and little ravines, and the air rushing past them feed whatever was now eating at him. He knew Isabella was different, that she wouldn't react the same way Scarlett had, but that didn't ease the anger he suddenly felt at finding he wasn't good enough for a normal woman to want.

It wasn't anything against Isabella, Apollo assured himself. She was hardly in a place to even understand what a man needed or felt. She was a freaking baby, for cripes sakes!

Apollo stopped abruptly, throwing Isabella against him. It was in his nature to apologize, to be a gentleman. But this overwhelming anger strangling him was too strong and refused to subside. Nothing he was feeling was normal. Everything in him had turned aggressive and hungry. Even though aware the thoughts bombarding him were wrong, he couldn't settle down.

He jumped from the four-wheeler and threw off the helmet, ignoring the cracking sound when it landed hard. The stunned look in Isabella's eyes should have been enough to stop him, but unknown demons drove him, consumed him, and would not be denied. Apollo pulled her off the idling machine and fought the helmet from her head. Her gasp and struggles didn't even penetrate until he'd planted his lips on hers, as one victorious in war would a flag.

The anger dispensated as her struggles did, but Apollo could only gentle the assault on her mouth. Damning himself, damning her, he couldn't yet release her, as her taste and texture flooded his senses, and ultimately, tamed what had taken him over. He leaned his forehead against hers when he could finally break the kiss, as shame flooded every part of his soul.

"I'm sorry."

Isabella said nothing, only continued to stare at him, and being so close he could see there was no fright in the violet eyes, only a waiting he couldn't read. "You get to slap me now."

That made her lips lift slightly, and her eyes sparkle with starbursts, as his mother's did whenever her magic activated. Knowing he had no idea what all Isabella was capable of, Apollo expected the slap to come in some form other than from her palm.

It was a surprise to feel those soft palms gently grasp his jaws, as she angled her head, and took his lips this time. Unlike his ravenous rage, her kiss was sweet, testing, and melted the last of his rabid energy. When their lips parted, she again studied his eyes.

"You did not need to get angry to kiss me."

Heat crept across his neck. "I'm sorry."

She nodded, but didn't release him. "You said that. But I'm not sure what it is you apologize for."

Apollo lifted his hands and loosely wrapped her in his arms. "For being a brute. For treating you as if I had a right to take you against your will. I am not that kind of man."

"I know you are not."

"So you'll forgive me?"

She studied him, her gaze as gentle as the breeze.

"There is nothing to forgive. I find I like kissing."

"Kissing can be fun, by itself, but it can also cause longings I don't believe you are ready to explore."

Her features altered, and Apollo knew she considered his words, but he couldn't tell how she took them.

"You think I'm dumb."

It wasn't a question, nor was it said with hurt or anger, but Apollo needed to clarify. "I don't think you are dumb. I think you have led such a sheltered life, that you need to know more about the world, and about life in general. I am the first man to give you security, I think…."

At her nod, he continued, "And as such, you are feeling things for me that aren't necessarily the things you would want to feel for a man you'd want to kiss like that."

"How do you know what I feel?"

Apollo knew he was making a mess of this. "I think you feel you *need* me. There is a difference between needing someone and wanting them. A kiss, like we just shared, should come from wanting, not needing."

Isabella's brows pulled together. "I don't know if that's true. I needed to escape the life I led, but I wanted to as well, once Sara started showing me things I knew I'd never seen. They were the same."

"No, sweetheart, it isn't. You needed to escape because they were doing you wrong and endangering you. You wanted to escape because you came to realize there was more beyond whatever gates they had you caged in. There are no boundaries for you here, but the ones you erect. Feeling that you owe me something, *anything*, which you do not, is another one of those boundaries."

"I need you to teach me."

"Teach you what?"

Isabella glanced around them, and she grinned when

her gaze again landed on his. "Everything."

Chapter Nine

Sara chewed slowly, relived they were finally allowing her to spend time alone. Two days of fear had passed since she'd last been assaulted, and she was finally able to swallow the broth with tiny vegetables without it all wanting to come back up her throat.

She hurt worse with each new day but knew they'd been careful enough not to break more than a few teeth and her arm. It didn't help the pain spearing the rest of her body, but it gave her hope. Her legs still worked, her mind was functioning better, and as long as they didn't find Izzy, she still could dream of escape.

That was her biggest fear, Sara decided. If they found the girl, there was no need for them to keep Sara, herself, alive. She knew they thought of her as nothing but a threat now, because that's exactly what she was.

She knew they were aware she had no close family ties, and that no one locally would miss her if she disappeared, since she'd had to put all her relationships down on the employment contract she'd signed. It should have been a red flag, she knew *now*, because she'd never worked anywhere else that asked so many personal questions or demanded she live on the property where she worked. But she'd wanted the money they offered and had pushed past the unease she'd felt while filling out all those forms.

It bit into her, knowing greed was what had placed her in her current predicament, but she hadn't known such a horrible place existed until she'd signed her life away. And she hadn't known there were other children being tested as

Izzy was, until she'd helped the girl escape at the end of her last session.

Why she'd spent the past two years allowing others to dictate her very restricted movements, made no sense now. Except she'd planned to take care of her charge for only a couple more years, before leaving the compound to start a new life with enough money to carry her for years.

Growing up in poverty, losing her parents when she was barely out of her teens, and scrounging and scraping to survive all the years since, made what The Barnabas Group representative had offered look too good to pass up. Of course, she hadn't known his real purpose at first. She'd been blinded by a need to be wanted. To be desired. To be someone's somebody, after so many years of struggling on her own.

It was no wonder she'd fallen prey.

Nothing in her life had prepared her for the attentions of an attractive well-dressed man, who smiled at her constantly and found reasons to call her over to take care of the most mundane of his needs. His kind didn't stop in at shabby roadside restaurants, nor did they return night after night to single-out someone like her as their personal waitress. She'd mistaken his interest as personal. And she, who never had dreamed of better than what was her lot in life, dreamed and dreamed big. It wasn't until he took the time to expound on the wonderful job opportunity he had for her, and then coaxed her into signing the non-disclosure papers, that she realized he'd been out fishing, and she was the catch.

Only she'd had no idea, even then, what it was she'd signed up, for.

"You done yet?"

Sara lilted her head so she could see which one had come to torment her. It was the fattest, which was a relief. He seemed a little retarded, and as far as she knew, he hadn't been one of the men hitting her. "I am."

She held out the soup with her good arm, knowing she should have eaten more to build her strength, but she didn't want them to think her too well of mind and body. If they did, she was afraid they'd come back and kick her around just for the fun of it.

"Boss says I'm to give you a shower."

Everything within her cringed, but Sara only nodded. She hadn't bathed since this all began. She was covered in dried blood, and she feared worse. If she could get past this chunk of lard seeing her naked, she hoped she'd feel a little better. "My arm."

He took the bowl from her and set it aside. "Doc said to wrap it in plastic and tape it up. As long as we don't get the cast wet, it will be fine."

Sara felt her good arm being pulled, and she struggled to stand. "If you will tape up my arm, I can shower myself."

There was a moment's hesitation on his part, and Sara's hope soared. Then he moved in front of her good eye, shaking his fat head.

"Boss says I'm to do it."

There was no point in arguing. She knew it, and slow as he was, he probably did too. Sara also knew she couldn't afford to balk, regardless. One word that she wasn't meekly complying, and the brutes would be sent back in to straighten her out, and she feared how they would handle her. At least with this one, she had a chance to get through the shower with nothing more than her dignity destroyed.

Chapter Ten

Isabella sat quietly and read the book, relieved Sara had taught her to read. She wasn't very good at it yet since her former opportunities had been so limited, and she still had to sound out some words and ignore others, but she was learning about the history of the country she lived in.

Until Apollo had explained it, she hadn't even known what countries were. Or wars, for that matter.

Although the words sometimes confused her, the pictures were nice and, at times, helpful. Colorful drawings of men in red coats and others without them portrayed the words she read. The men not in red fought those that were, so this land could become its own country. If she understood correctly, they'd all once come from a place called England, and like her, their lives hadn't been their own to live as they pleased. *And* like her, they'd found a way to escape, only to still have threats hanging over their heads.

Given the results of such violent behavior, this war seemed somewhat polite. Both sides marched slowly forward in groups of men that never fell out of line even when someone died, while others in their army played drums and an instrument called a fife. Isabella couldn't imagine any of it. Especially since these lines of men pointed at each other with long guns, which shot little balls that could injure or kill, and they had knives sticking out the front of the weapons, which they stabbed each other with. Yet the music wasn't to stop. If a player fell, someone was supposed to pick up his instrument and march on. She couldn't decide if they were very brave or very stupid.

"That isn't entirely accurate, but it gives you the gist of things."

Isabella looked up and smiled, happy to see Apollo had returned from his run. "Gist?"

"An idea. An overall impression."

She nodded. "I see. If it's wrong, why did you give it to me to read?"

Apollo hesitated only a minute. "Because it's what we were taught in public school when we were younger."

Isabella looked at the book again, figuring he meant when he was very young. Her ignorance about everything she *should have been taught* all these year was becoming an embarrassment.

"It isn't your fault, Isabella. Those people took your life and gave you nothing in return. And you're doing great. Before you know it, you'll be up to speed."

Gratitude, which he didn't want from her, was always there, and it increased with each kindness. There was no way she could take his thoughtfulness for granted, but she knew the gratitude was to be hers to carry in silence.

"It just makes me feel like a child. And I shouldn't be one at this point in my life."

He nodded. "No, they robbed you. But you can change that. You can defeat them by taking control of your life and education, and I'm here to help anytime you want it."

The idea she could overcome all that was once denied was empowering, but even that wasn't what settled so heavily in Isabella's chest. She'd seen the interactions of his cousins with their spouses, and she knew, after the kisses she and Apollo shared the day before, learning from books was only a small part of growing up. The girl talk had been confusing, until she'd experienced that first rough kiss. It still was to some degree. She felt she'd have to participate in the other things the women spoke of before she understood any of it better.

Isabella set *The History of Our Nation* aside and rose to stretch. She'd been reading for what seemed hours, while Apollo had scanned the surrounding area for danger.

Before departing the cabin earlier, he'd said he just wanted to take a run to exercise. Seconds later, with a frown, Apollo added he also wanted to make sure there were no strangers close by. She'd appreciated his honesty, even though his words served to remind her that her ordeal might never be over. She'd almost begged him to stay close but held the shameful plea inside. She didn't want to let him know what a coward she was. It was embarrassing enough to acknowledge it to herself.

Once alone, she'd been too tightly wound to focus on her assignment, had in fact read the first page many times over. As time when on, Isabella settled in, but the complete silence often served to pull her attention from the book, and she'd find herself staring at the door.

Not sure how long he'd actually been gone, but thinking it much longer than she'd first expected, Isabella was glad she'd nearly finished the little book, otherwise she'd have to admit how scared she'd been. Relieved he was back and seemed unworried, Isabella determined not to let fear rule her life the next time she was left alone. She smiled up at him, hoping it looked as if she didn't have a care in the world.

"When do we go to your parents' house?"

"In about an hour. Do you need anything before then?"

She wanted to kiss him again. To feel those stirrings within. But he hadn't initiated the contact since the beginning of their ride the day before, so she was afraid it wasn't what he wanted. Isabella shook her head, and her long blond hair swung forward to lie across her shoulders and chest. She grabbed it all and made quick work of braiding it as Sara had taught her to do.

"You have beautiful hair. It's the color of sun-bleached wheat right before harvest."

The complement was unexpected and warmed her. "Thank you."

"The rest of you isn't so bad either."

Since she believed there was teasing in his voice, she took that as a compliment as well. "You look like a younger version of your father. He is a beautiful man."

Apollo's lips quivered, before he smiled. "Does that make me a beautiful man as well?"

Having never felt the shyness overcoming her now, Isabella wasn't sure what to do with it, but she nodded. She expected honesty from him, and could give back nothing else. "Yes."

Apollo looked uncertain for only seconds before he moved closer.

"Isabella…"

He shook his head and turned away.

Disappointment flooded her, as she'd been certain he'd wanted to kiss her. "Apollo!"

Her hasty shout made him turn back, but he only grinned at her and headed for the kitchen.

"If you're ready to go, I'm sure my parents wouldn't mind us arriving a little early."

All the things she wanted to say fled in the light of his response. "Sure."

Less than a half an hour later, they were again pulling into the long drive, only this time it was of less interest to her. She didn't look to her right to see if any of Sapphire's Lycanthrope family hovered near. All she could think of was the low hum in the middle of her stomach, which had nothing to do with hunger for the meal to come.

Something was happening to her, had awakened within

her, and she knew it was directly related to Apollo. She hated the space between, not just that of the truck's seat. She wanted him to reach out to her, to invite her closer, so they could hold hands while he drove. She craved that special look he sometimes sent her, and hated when he'd look away quickly and make himself busy doing something else.

She knew she wasn't his equal on any level, and that, more than anything, was what kept Isabella from asking for all the things she wanted so badly.

"We're here."

She looked up to find his parents standing on the porch, and both joy and trepidation held her immobile when he stopped. He was out of his door and at hers before she could blink, and he finally held her hand as she alit from the truck.

Destiny's smile was big, Tom's welcoming, and Isabella hoped her own smile was as well. She was happy to see them again, but she felt as though she'd grown years since the day before, and only now realized how pitiful she must look to them all.

Not letting her feelings show, she returned the warm greetings sent her way. This time when Destiny kissed each of her cheeks, there was concern in those green eyes when she pulled back. She sent Apollo and Tom a meaningful look, though Isabella had no idea what it meant.

Since they both said something about a video game and hurried down the hall leading to the large family room she'd been shown the day before, she could only surmise that had been Destiny's doing. She followed the older woman to the kitchen. Afraid something uncomfortable was to come, she quickly asked, "Is there anything I can do to help?"

Destiny shook her head. "No, everything is just finishing up. I thought we could just have a few minutes to ourselves and give the guys a chance to catch up." She grinned. "We don't see our boys all that often now that they're grown. Not even Apollo, even though he lives and works so close."

She chewed on her bottom lip and looked down to her hands, before looking again into Isabella's eyes. "You are sad. Is my son not making you happy?"

Feeling it a betrayal to Apollo to have his mother think such a thing had her nodding enthusiastically. "He is kindness. He's wonderful in every way. He would never do anything to make me unhappy."

Destiny nodded. "I know he wouldn't on purpose. But there is sadness in you, and I feel it's because of my son."

Because she'd never had the opportunity to talk to a mother of her own, Isabella wasn't sure if it was even appropriate for her to share her deepest feelings and thoughts with Destiny. Although Apollo's mother seemed open to discussing her son's shortcoming, Isabella knew the problem didn't lie with him.

"It's me…"

Destiny tilted her head. "What is, sweetheart?"

Isabella couldn't help but be disheartened. "Just like you talking to me now. You call me sweetheart."

Destiny stared at her. "If you don't like it, I can stop."

Shaking her head, knowing she wasn't making sense, Isabella forged on. "It isn't that I don't like it. I think it's lovely that you call me that. It's just the reason for you talking to me so gently, when you don't others. I know I'm uneducated, and I'm ignorant of just about everything, but I am not a child!

"You talk to me the way you talk to Jewell's children."

Destiny nodded slowly. "I'm sorry. I didn't realize I was doing that. It's just that I'm an Intuit and can read people, and your heart is as pure as that of a child." She reached forward as if to touch Isabella's hand, then she pulled it back. "I am so sorry. I'll be more careful. I would never mean to do anything to make you feel bad."

Isabella sighed. "Now I've made *you* feel bad. I didn't mean to do that either."

Destiny smile took several seconds to build, but with it, understanding entered her eyes. "You are having feelings you don't understand?"

Surprised by the change of subject, Isabella shrugged, and then nodded. "Yes."

Nodding, Destiny settled against the countertop, and leaned back to look Isabella over. "About my son. About the kind of relationship we talked about yesterday?"

Certain the heat in her cheeks meant they'd filled with pink color, Isabella glanced toward the hallway the men had taken. "And since he kissed me out in the woods."

Destiny's eyebrows shot up. "Ah… He kissed you."

Isabella nodded, relieved, if still somewhat embarrassed, to be talking to his mother about such things. But she had to talk to someone! "It did something to me."

Destiny laughed. "When it's the right guy, it always does."

At Isabella's frown she continued. "Look, sweet— *Isabella*. The attraction between men and women is always tricky, and scary, and hard to negotiate. But, Apollo, being Apollo, will give you whatever time you need to figure out whatever it is that you're feeling."

"What if it isn't what *you* want it to be?"

Destiny looked taken aback, and Isabella would do nothing but wait for her response.

"What is it you think I want?" Destiny asked.

Truly uncomfortable, and hoping she wasn't making a complete fool of herself, Isabella took a deep breath and released it. "I think you want me to have sex with him."

To Isabella's horror, Destiny threw her head back and laughed. When she sobered, she was shaking her head and then nodding, only confusing Isabella more.

"Well, of course I do! But not until you fall in love with him."

There was no way to explain this, except to state it outright. "I don't know how to do that."

"Oh, sweetheart!" Destiny wrinkled her nose. "I'm sorry, but that's what you are to me, so please forgive me if I slip up and call you sweetheart. Just know it isn't because I think of you as a child. You mean something to my soul...whether you end up with my son or not."

Isabella smiled. "I can live with that."

"Good. Now, what I was about to say, *sweetheart*, is that you don't ever know how to fall in love. It just happens."

"How do you know when you do then?"

Destiny shrugged. "Sometimes, like with me and Tom, your souls reach for each other before you even meet. And when you do meet, you know that person is the one. My sisters both had different experiences. Haven was wild about Logan when she first met him, but she fought it and him, and they ended up having quite a time of it. And then Rayne, and Garrison, I think their love bloomed slowly. They struggled through a time that was very difficult for his family. Rayne was trying to help out, while trying as hard not to expose her gift. By the time they got to know each other on one level, her true self became apparent. And she found he loved her still.

"But all that is a story for another day. The long and short of it is this: for each of us, finding love is complicated and unique, and if it is true, that love will run deep for an eternity, just as it has for my sisters and myself."

"That's great. But it takes two people. I have no idea if I'd recognize it if it happened, and I don't think Apollo is interested in me that way. I think he thinks of me as a...little sister, maybe?"

Distaste covered Destiny's features. "Why in the world

do you think he feels *that* way about you?"

Isabella shrugged. "He brought me all kinds of books to read so I could learn the things he learned as a child. And he stays away from me when...*I guess*...he can tell I want him to kiss me again."

Chuckling, Destiny shook her head. "That son of mine! Don't you worry about any of this, sweetheart. If you really want him to kiss you again, initiate it yourself. There are no rules. You don't have to wait for him to get his head out of the past."

As if realizing she'd said something she shouldn't have, Destiny glanced toward the hallway before turning back and leaning into Isabella. "He was in love once, and the girl was all over him. He fell hard, and when he thought he could trust her to share his ability to run, she dumped him and told him he was nothing more than a freak. It got to be bigger than that, but the important thing is how it injured him."

Indignation rose up inside Isabella. "That's terrible!"

Destiny nodded. "It is, but it is also expected, which is why we are all so careful about exposing ourselves to outsiders. The girl went to her parents, and before long, it was all over town. Fortunately, no one believed her, but it was a big lesson for us all."

"I bet he felt bad for bringing all that attention to you all."

Destiny nodded. "I know he did, though he shouldn't have. But Apollo was young. There was nothing we could say to change the way he felt about the family being questioned so publicly. We had to let time take care of it, as well as his broken heart. It took him years to get over that girl, or at least we think it did. The truth is we can only speculate, because he never again mentioned her. But he did stop using his gifts. Until you came along, I don't think he ever planned to use them again."

Chapter Eleven

Sara stared straight ahead, determined not to cry out. The concrete block wall was mere inches from her face. She knew it would take only one firm push on this beast's part and her face would meet it hard.

She'd tried to ignore his hands all over her when he bathed her the day before and had even kept herself from crying out when he'd pushed two slick fingers inside, but that hadn't been enough for him. He was back again today, and this time it wasn't to give her a shower or simply feel her up.

Chapter Twelve

Apollo tried to concentrate on Ryan Steward's latest video game, but his father was kicking his butt, because he couldn't.

"You're head's not in this."

He glanced over at his father and nodded, before taking the hands-free gear from his head and moving the electronic device onto his lap.

"Mom is interfering."

Tom shrugged. "That's her way. Nothing says you have to allow it."

Apollo chewed at his upper lip and shook his head. "I don't have a say. If Isabella wants to talk to her about…*stuff*, that's their business."

Tom smiled. "You're just afraid of you mother."

Apollo laughed. "Aren't you?"

"Your mother doesn't try to control me. She likes to please me."

Apollo knew that to be true. His father was too in tune with himself and the world to become a target of their mother's manipulations. It was good to know someone was immune to her tongue. But as his father insinuated, he wasn't that someone.

"I'm a grown ass man."

Tom rarely barked out anything, but he did a laugh now. "Yes, you are."

"Destiny Cavanaugh-Whitehawk shouldn't be in there trying to determine my fate!"

"No," Tom agreed. "She shouldn't. Which is why I'm

wondering why you're in here getting your butt wiped on the floor, and they are in there."

Apollo pushed to his feet, but only to pace the large room he and his brothers played in growing up. On his second pass, he looked down at his father, irritated the elder was so content to watch him squirm. "Isabella is important to me."

Tom grinned. "That's good to know."

"It's just that I don't know how to handle her. She's a child!"

Tom's brows shot up, and the smile left his lips. "She's hardly that."

Apollo began pacing again, his feet moving fast with each lap. Tom sat up a little straighter. "You're going to wear a path in your mother's floor, and then you'll really need to be scared of her."

Taking a deep breath, Apollo slowed, stopping again when he reached his father's chair. "She doesn't know anything!"

"Destiny?"

"Isabella!"

"So teach her."

Irritated his father never raised his voice or lost his cool, Apollo made himself calm down, and he took the same gaming seat he'd vacated moments before. "I am teaching her. Or at least providing the tools for her to learn."

"I know you are, but I didn't mean that. Teach her to want you."

Apollo looked at his father in surprise. "You can't teach someone that."

Tom laid his head back and closed his eyes. "Sure you can. You're a handsome enough fellow." Tom rolled his head to the side and peeked at his son with one eye, laughed, and turned back so his nose was again up in the air, and both eyes closed.

"Funny, Dad."

Tom shrugged. "Just saying."

"Now you sound like Heracles and Zeus."

"And you."

Apollo thought about it for a second and had to concede. "Okay, like me too. But that's not the point!"

Tom lifted his head and turned Apollo's way. "So, what's the point?"

"I'm so much older than she is."

"Wrong tactic. I'm a lot older than your mother, more than you are Isabella, and I can still satisfy her in bed…or the floor…or—"

Apollo held up his hand. "Okay! Got it, Dad. I don't need a list of the places you nail my mother."

Tom laughed. "Sons."

There was no reason to question his father's single word. He and his brothers had made themselves scares too many times to count when Tom and Destiny Whitehawk got a certain look in their eyes for each other. It was the biggest reason this large room had been added to the original structure, back when he and his brothers were kids.

Soundproofed when the doors were closed, and so large all kinds of juvenile play could take place, this room was a refuge for the young Whitehawk boys. It not only accommodated their needs when they were forced to stay indoors, it kept them from hearing all the rocking and rolling going on in the rest of the log structure when their parents forgot anyone existed except each other.

Which had been often, and for long spans of time.

The ground rules of no parental sex taking place where they themselves played had been dictated by the brothers early on, and Tom and Destiny had agreed they'd leave this room free from their lusty shenanigans… At least until the boys grew up and moved out.

Realizing just how many years ago that actually was, Apollo let out a sigh. He wasn't getting any younger, and he wanted sons, or daughters, of his own. And now that Isabella had awakened something in him, lots of lusty shenanigans too.

"She's got good hips."

Apollo sent a glare to his father. "Mom does that, please, not you too."

"Just saying they'd loosen up to pop out some fine babies."

"Dad, *seriously*."

"You're still young and strong and have my genes, so there's that as well."

"Dad, I've never hit you before."

Tom grinned at him. "Don't think this old man couldn't take you, if push came to shove."

"Since there is no way we are going to find out, stop."

Tom rested his head back again. "I think after having you boys, your mom would like little girls."

Apollo's head fell forward. "I concede. Do you want me to drag her into my old room and do the deed tonight so everyone will be happy?" he asked, certain it was the first time in his twenty-five years he'd ever sassed his father.

The feel of his father's big hand landing on his forearm caused Apollo to look over. "What?"

"All kidding aside, we want *you* to be happy. You crave her?"

Apollo nodded slowly. "I do."

Tom's smile was one of satisfaction. "Then pursue her at whatever pace you're both comfortable with."

"I don't want my Cavanaugh genes to dictate my life."

"Ah, *the claiming*. Your Whitehawk genes are just as strong in you as the Cavanaugh, and we, on both sides, only *crave* the one we were meant to have all along." After a brief pause, Tom pulled his hand back and sat up straighter in his chair. "If you feel those cravings as deeply as I believe you do, she was meant to be yours, and as importantly, you were meant to be hers."

Apollo wanted to believe it, but he'd wanted another at one time. Before he could remind his father of that fiasco, Tom shook his head.

"You were a young man with raging hormones and mistook lust for love."

Not surprised he would never hold a secret of his own, since both of his parents were mystics who could see into others souls, Apollo gave up and stood, ready to take charge of his own life. He turned back once. "How can you be so sure she's the one?"

Tom leaned back into his seat again, complete contentment on his face. "How can you not?"

****

Relieved dinner ended up a relaxed affair, and Isabella looked *none the worse for wear* after having spent so much time alone with his mother, Apollo was more than ready to head home four hours into their visit. Hugs and kisses abounded, and final goodbyes kept being thwarted when someone had one more thing they needed to say, so it was very late when he and Isabella were finally on their way.

Isabella leaned back in the truck's seat and hummed to the country song playing on the radio. Apollo smiled over at her, knowing he'd have to introduce her to his eclectic music collection and let her decide what she liked.

"Did you have a good time?"

Her head lolled in his direction, and a smile tilted her lips. "I had a great time. Your parents are wonderful."

Her own was a subject he'd never broached. Apollo was hesitant to do so now, with Isabella looking so pleased with her life, but after a short internal debate, he knew he had to ask. "Did you ever know your own?"

She shook her head. "No."

"Have you ever wondered about them?"

She nodded. "But only after meeting yours."

He left it there, deciding it was up to her if she wanted to continue talking about them. When she said nothing more, he drove the distance to his own driveway and then realized there were headlights coming around the curve behind him.

Not wanting to alarm her, Apollo said nothing as he passed it by and continued up the mountain road. He waited for her to comment about how long it was taking to return to their home, but one quick glance proved her asleep. He reached across the cab with his free hand and undid her seatbelt before pulling her down so her head lay against his thigh. She made a little sound of contentment, and he couldn't help the responding sigh.

Giving his attention to those following, he was relieved moments later to see the truck pulling into one of his Whitehawk cousin's driveways. More relaxed, he went as far as he needed to turn into another of his cousin's gravel lanes, before lowering his headlights. Using only the low beam of the running lights to turn the truck around, he returned to the entry and stopped. Apollo placed the truck in park long enough to rearrange Isabella so her back wasn't twisted. She looked uncomfortable to him, and he didn't want her to return to their cabin in pain.

"Are we home?"

Apollo looked down and smiled at her dash light-illuminated face. Her beauty stole his breath, and he knew if he were a contortionist, her lips would belong to his instantly. "We will be in a few minutes. Just stay there, and rest."

"Mmm-kay."

Her sleepy response made him think of black satin sheets, which was funny since he owned none. Determined to get them home quickly, and her safely away from him tucked into her own bed, he put the truck back into gear, and looked up. The white light reflecting off the trees to his right had him scrambling to turn his own completely off.

He sat in the darkness, wishing he'd stopped a little further back in the driveway, as he waited, knowing he was probably being paranoid. But one other vehicle on the road at this time of night he could ignore. Two, was stretching it. The locals were all from one side or the other of his family, and in nearly every case, they were *early to bed and early to rise* kind of people.

Apollo licked his lips as the car approached, and he looked as hard as he could into the driver's window as it passed. The car's lit dashboard clearly outlined the faces and shoulders of two men, making him take another moment before he started his truck's engine again.

Of course, it could mean nothing, but he wasn't taking any chances.

Apollo pulled out once the other vehicle was completely out of sight and headed with more speed than he normally used all the way back to his hidden drive. He went over the hills and valleys he'd driven for years, for the first time thinking the drive long. As soon as he stopped before his home, Apollo turned off lights and engine and then took a moment to sit looking around. The sight of Jaspon prowling the grounds sent relief through his body. He nodded to the werewolf, and the wolf nodded back, before he bound into the trees.

Knowing Isabella safe for now, Apollo opened his door and eased from beneath her slumbering head. He left her long enough to unlock the front door and prop it open with one of the porch chairs before returning to lift her and pull her from the truck.

Giggles filled and tickled his ear.

"I can walk, you know."

Figuring the wine his mother poured at dinner had as

much to do with her exhaustion as the hours of the long day, Apollo held her close. "I've got you."

She leaned forward and kissed his cheek. "Yes, you do."

Grinning, he turned her sideways to take her through the front door. "My mother shouldn't have let you drink. You're underage. And you're drunk."

Another kiss on the cheek. "I'm not drunk. Your mom explained what that was while you were talking to your dad. But I do feel so loose, which is kind of fun. And it tasted good. Besides, she only let me have one glass with that incredible meal."

"How would you know if you were drunk?" Apollo asked, setting her feet on the floor, before he reached back and shut the door. She leaned into him and smiled into his face when he turned back her way.

"Okay. Maybe I am a little. But it's so relaxing."

Isabella slid her arms around Apollo's waist, and he had to consciously stop himself from wrapping her in his embrace. "You should go to bed."

A deep chuckle came with the shake of her head. "You should kiss me."

There was no way he was biting on that. "Not tonight. If you still want me to in the morning, I will then."

Isabella pouted, and the sight of those pursed lips made him lick his own. Still, he wasn't going to take advantage of her, under *any* circumstances.

"You don't want to kiss me?"

Knowing he had to get her out of his arms and into her bed as soon as possible, he shook his head. "Not after you've been drinking."

She smiled at him lazily, teasingly. "You think you won't like the taste of my lips?"

Apollo steeled himself. "I would like the taste of your lips just fine. I just don't want you to regret tonight, tomorrow."

Isabella giggled. "Your mom says you're too much of a gentleman." She frowned. "After she explained what one was, she said it stifles you."

"My mother says too much, but I've been called worse."

Isabella pressed herself against him tighter, and Apollo loudly cleared the knot forming in his throat.

"She said I should make you kiss me when I wanted to."

Since he hadn't had the opportunity for that private talk with his mother, Apollo knew he'd have to make sure it happened the next time they were together. Which needed to be soon. This had to stop.

"You shouldn't be taking advice from my mother about kissing me."

Isabella dropped her hands and stepped back. She looked up at him, hurt in her eyes.

"Do you really not want to kiss me?"

Apollo almost snorted, but caught himself. "Of course I want to kiss you. But I'm not going to do it because my mother says so."

"She only told me that because I told her I wanted you to, but you wouldn't."

The thing about complete honesty was it was uncomfortable at times…like now. Apollo debated and then decided he had no choice but to lay it all out to her. "You're young. You're inexperienced. And I won't rush you into something you'll regret once you have a better understanding of who you are. You haven't gotten a chance to know yourself yet."

"You've said that. But why would I regret it?" she asked and then swayed.

Apollo moved forward and grabbed her to steady her, only to have her throw herself against him again. Her high breasts teased his abdomen, her slim hips the top of his thighs. He inhaled deeply as his body sprung to life, but he couldn't push her away. He held her tightly, allowing the growing bulge in his jeans to press against her.

"Do you feel that?"

Isabella's eyes opened wide, and she nodded.

"That's me, wanting you."

She shivered in his arms but didn't look away. "Your penis."

He nodded, thinking this had to be the worst possible way for a man his age to deal with a woman he desperately wanted. "Yes. That's how a man's body reacts when he wants to take a woman's body."

She grinned. "So you do want me."

"You're not ready for that yet."

She nodded slowly. "You're mom said it is better when two people are in love, and I'm sure she knows what she's talking about. But she doesn't know how it makes me feel when you kiss me and hold me like you are now."

Thinking of his unapologetic very sexual mother, he almost laughed, but didn't. "I'm sure she knows *exactly* how you feel. You're a young woman whose hormones have awakened, and you're curious, as is normal. But you are under my protection, and I can't give into the wanting, until I know you know exactly what you're getting into.

"Having sex complicates even an already established, mature, relationship. You and I need to get to know each other, and like I said, you don't even know yourself yet."

She released him and stepped back, anger swirling in her eyes.

"You think I'm a kid. I get that. But you need to get something too. I've been denied everything my entire life. I'm not afraid to learn *anything*. I want to know what every other nineteen year old girl already knows, and I want to learn it from someone I trust!"

Apollo didn't know what to say. How had this turned from him wanting to take her on a slow journey to discovering love, to her expecting him to be nothing but a sex education teacher? He shook his head, his own anger building to match hers.

"You don't know what you're asking!"

"That's why I want you to teach me!"

"It isn't just physical! It will affect you emotionally!"

Isabella shook her head, the anger in her eyes darts into his soul. He wanted to make this about her and her needs, but he knew he'd built a wall around his heart years ago to protect himself from hurt, a wall she'd begun to dismantle. Apollo backed away, afraid too much damage to that sturdy structure was already crumbling to erect it again. But he was determined to try.

"Go to bed, Isabella!"

She shook her head. "Make me!"

Her defiance was as new to him as the display of anger, and it only fed the frustration of years of enforced self-denial. Apollo advanced and clasped her arm before dragging her to his room. Isabella went without struggle, but when he released her, she smacked his cheek hard.

Apollo was as stunned as she looked, but it did nothing to dispense the rage within. "Go. To. Bed!"

Isabella put her hands to the button-down opening of the summer dress Sapphire had given her, and grasped each side and pulled. Buttons flew as she flung the dress open and Apollo was certain his jaw dropped when the black lace bra and hip-hugging panties revealed firm breasts and a body as toned as his own. He looked her up and down, and his rage slipped and slid into something more.

Furious still that she continued to defy him, he advanced on her. "You want *this* that bad? *Fine!*"

Apollo ripped the rest of the dress from her shoulders, and unhooked her bra in one quick flick of his fingers. Her gasps only increase his anger, as he pulled the bra away, and then jerked her panties down to her knees. He let them fall the rest of the way as he lifted Isabella and dumped her on the bed. With hyper-quick speed, his own body was bared as well, and he was at her side before she could even roll away.

The taste of her lips as he ravaged them, the feel of her softness against the hard length of him, penetrated the rage, and the realization that she was fighting him finally brought him to his senses. He pulled back quickly ready to beg her forgiveness, only to hear the loud crash at the front of the house.

Apollo was on his feet instantly, ready to do battle with any who had come to do Isabella harm, but dropped his fists and could only stare when a heaving Sapphire transformed into her human form. She stood in the doorway as proud as always, her nude form a masterpiece of the species into which she was originally born. She looked from Apollo to Isabella and then back at him again.

"Just what the hell have you done?"

Chapter Thirteen

"What the *hell* have you done!"

Sara lay in a sobbing heap, unable to look to see who had come into the room to yell at *her rapist*. The big man had torn her apart, and she could only remain curled into the bloody ball she had become.

"You idiot! Mr. Barnabas is going to kill you!"

"I wanted to fuck her normal, but I couldn't make it work."

There was silence before the other man sighed. "Get the hell out of here before someone else comes. I'll take care of this mess."

"Thank you, Bubby. I'm sorry. Please don't be mad."

"I'm not mad. But you are going to be in big trouble if this woman dies. Just go home. I'll be there later."

Sara held her breath to stop the sobbing and remained frozen in place as she digesting the little information the exchange provided. As much as she hurt, knowing she wasn't supposed to be harmed any more than the initial beatings, at least until they found Izzy, helped.

She rolled over when the big hand on her shoulder forced her too. Since the swelling had gone down some on her injured eye, Sara was able to see out of both, although her vision was still too blurry to make out exact features, and the addition of tears only made it worse.

"I'm sorry. He doesn't know what he did."

Sara almost emitted a laugh, but it came out in another sob. That this man thought her being brutally raped by that buffoon as something to apologize for, given what had already been done to her, almost seemed comical.

Almost.

"You report this, and I'll kill you myself and make it look like suicide."

Of course, the other man meant something to him. He didn't give a shit about her.

"I won't tell," she promised, knowing it for truth. No one here would really care anyway.

"Smart girl. Now turn over and let me see what I'm dealing with."

Sara made a real effort to stop the tears and do as he'd demanded, not even caring now. It wasn't as if she had a choice anyway.

When he swore, she sighed. He didn't have to tell her that the other man had messed her up bad.

"I'll wash you down, and get the doc in here to sew you up, but you breathe a word about who did this, and I ain't kidding, I'll silence you for good."

Chapter Fourteen

Sapphire pushed Apollo out of her way as she rushed to Isabella's side and dropped to her knees at the edge of the bed. He turned to find she'd magically clothed herself, and remembered his own state of undress. Lost in a fog of self-disgust, he fumbled his way into covering himself again. It took much longer than when divesting his clothes, but once he was done, he walked to where Sapphire was and looked down at the teary-eyed girl he had wronged.

"Isabella, I'm sorry."

Before Isabella could turn from the whispered conversation she and his cousin were having, Sapphire rose, blocking her as if a shield, and glared at him. "The living room. Now!"

The urge to tell his cousin to mind her own business and get lost, froze on Apollo's lips when Isabella turned her body away, refusing to look at him.

He glanced back to Sapphire and nodded. "Okay."

Apollo pulled the door closed behind him and slowly made his way to the room where his cousin stood waiting like the regal Lycanthrope queen she was. Her look was one of disbelief as well as dismay. He understood. But he had no idea how any of them had come to this point.

"Why are you here?"

Sapphire blinked in surprise. "*That* is what you have to say?"

Apollo headed to the kitchen, in desperate need of a drink. Unfortunately, he never had anything but water on hand, so it would have to do. He snagged a bottle for himself and one for his cousin as well. Without a word, he threw it at her, and as expected, she caught it with one hand, twisted off the top, and downed it as quickly as he did his own.

"Answer me."

Sapphire moved to the kitchen, pitched her bottle into the recycle container, and then settled her back against the counter. "Your mother telepathically sent me a message to get over here with all haste. She didn't say why, but her distress was clear. Now I can see why."

She looked him over, confusion in her sapphire eyes.

"*Why*, Apollo? Why would you treat that girl so roughly?"

There was no excuse for what he'd done, and he offered none. "I lost it. I don't know how to explain what happened, except to say that.

"I don't blame her for hating me. Isabella's right to place *all* the blame on me."

Sapphire shook her head. "That's just it. She doesn't. Not at all. She said she made you angry, and she deserved what happened. But after you threw her on the bed she realized you weren't yourself, and it frightened her."

Apollo frowned. "It isn't her fault. None of it. I have to tell her that."

Sapphire nodded. "Yes, you do. But you need to figure out what happened first. I've never seen you angry before. I doubt anyone has. What set you off?"

It took a moment of self-exploration before Apollo could settle on a theory. "I convinced myself Isabella was what everyone else seems to think she is to me, but I couldn't reconcile that with what she is. She's only now discovering her sexuality, as well as everything else, but with her, I don't want to be a teacher to a student. I want to be a man to a woman. A lover. Who is wanted just because she is as lost in discovery as I am, and I'm the only one she believes will satisfy her."

The tilt of Sapphire's head indicated she was processing his words. They'd always been closer to each other than their respective siblings and other cousins, and it was comforting to know the way she ticked. Just as comforting, she knew him as intimately, too. Sapphire finally seemed to come to some decision, and then again looked at him, rather than through him.

"I think Isabella needs to come home with me for a while."

Denial slammed through Apollo, and he advanced on her before he realized it. He looked into her eyes, ready to tell her to go to hell, but he forced himself to stop. When he could finally catch his breath, and speak without anger, he searched her eyes again, this time, knowing she was right.

"For how long?"

Sapphire smiled and reached up to gently pat his cheek. "Not for long, cuz, I don't imagine. But you and Isabella need some time away from each other, and she needs time to process all the things she is experiencing as well.

"And, perhaps, she needs to see the way two people, who are in love, interact. She's never had the opportunity, as we did. We all grew up with parents who couldn't keep their hands off each other, but more importantly, we saw how they were when otherwise engaged. How they laughed at the same things and were angry over the same things. Everything *we* know about relationships, sexual or otherwise, was taught by example. Isabella has no point of reference. She may believe the way she expressed wanting you was the only way, but she has no idea what the right way is. Not even for her."

Apollo hung his head. "I hate it when you're smarter than I am."

Sapphire laughed and hugged him hard, and he returned it just as hard.

"I'm always smarter than you, you gorgeous hunk of man. Don't assume anything where she's concerned. She doesn't know what to do with what she's feeling much less understand any of it. The cousins and I can help there, some, too. We've all experienced some form of the same thing, even if we acted upon it differently. That first rush of hormones is confusing for a girl, as is that first attraction for a man. I would imagine she's so lost right now, the only reaction she could have is fear."

"And I made it worse by nearly raping her."

"You don't have rape in you, cuz. It never would have happened."

Relief washed through him. "Thank you, for saying that."

"It's only the truth."

Knowing she was right lifted weight from his shoulders, but there was more pushing against him. "But Isabella wouldn't know that."

Sapphire smiled. "She only feared your anger, not you."

Apollo sighed. "Take her home with you. And tell her I'm sorry, and I'll see her soon. Right now, I just can't face her. I need to take a run."

Sapphire opened her mouth then closed it without uttering the protest he knew she was about to give. Finally, she nodded, her eyes shining with amusement.

"You men are stupid creatures, but we can't seem to live without you. Go have your run, cuz, and I'll take care of your girl."

****

Isabella dressed slowly, unable to believe Apollo left without giving her a chance to apologize. She hadn't meant to make him angry... *Except* that she had.

Honesty with others was so much easier than with herself. She'd wanted to get a reaction out of him, and nothing had worked, until she'd demanded he teach her about physical love.

She'd spent an amazing evening with him, watching the laughter and love his parents displayed without thought. She saw the tiny fingertip touches as they passed each other, and the laughter they'd shared over the simplest things. She wanted to understand those secret, saucy, sassy glances Destiny sent to her husband, which made his eyes sparkle in response. She'd *felt* their love and desire for each other, as if it were a vital element making up the air. Through the entire evening, Isabella's thoughts fell back to the words of his female cousins from the day before. They knew how to lure their men into wanting to have sex, by simply expressing the desire. It all seemed so simple for the women of this amazing family. But hadn't worked for her on Apollo. He didn't want her as badly as she'd wanted him. It wasn't his fault she let her feelings get hurt. Or that hurt had turned to anger she'd had no idea how to control. And she couldn't blame him for not wanting to see her again, or have her live in his house.

He must hate me.

"Are you about ready to go?"

Isabella slipped into her shoes, and nodded. "I guess so."

"Are you okay?" Sapphire asked, coming farther into the room.

Was she? Isabella didn't know. "Yeah."

Sapphire lifted the small pile of clothing that was everything Isabella owned. Those, like the shoes, were all gifts from the woman settling at her side. Isabella looked at her clasped hands. "Was he still mad?"

Sapphires long-fingered right hand covered her own, causing Isabella to glance up and over her way. His cousin's face expressed concern.

"He is only angry with himself. He isn't violent, ever. Apollo would never hurt anyone, and he's sick that he treated you so roughly."

"It was my own fault."

Sapphire shook her head. "No. It wasn't. No matter what you did, he could have walked away. And he knows it. That he didn't is eating at him." Sapphire inhaled deeply. "Something you need to know about our beloved Apollo is he keeps himself on a tight leash. He never gets angry, raises his voice, or acts out in any way that isn't gentlemanly, well, except with his brothers, and that's only because it's the way they play."

Isabella frowned. "Isn't that a good thing?"

Sapphire shrugged. "If you're an angel, sure. For the rest of us it's almost impossible to maintain that kind of self-control all the time." She grinned. "You managed to unleash something primal in him, which is really kind of cool. It's nice to know he's as fallible as the rest of us. Now you need to think about what it is you want to do with all the power you hold."

Isabella bit her lip, not seeing it a power, but a failing on her part. She threw Sapphire another glance, uncertain what she'd meant. "You make it sound like all this is a good thing. It doesn't feel that way."

"I think it is. But don't worry about it for now. Let's get to my house and get to bed. It's been a long day, and tomorrow I want to show you how girls with the Cavanaugh genes like to relax. My sisters and cousins will be thrilled with a day at Mystic Manor Spa. Deep tissue massages, manicures and pedicures, and the facials are to die for. Are you game?"

Isabella nodded, having no idea what she was agreeing to. "Sure. Will Apollo be there?"

Sapphire grinned. "Absolutely not. No men. That's all

part of the fun."

Isabella rose and followed Sapphire from Apollo's house, to an idling truck she'd never seen before. The sight of Nicolae waiting behind the wheel made her feel more confused than ever. The women she'd met since coming to Mystic Mountain adored their men, loved spending time with them. Apparently, they liked having time away from them just as well. She waited until Sapphire was in the truck's cab and settled beside her husband, before climbing in herself.

Nicolae leaned forward, smiled at Isabella from around his wife, and then threw the truck into reverse. Isabella looked straight ahead at the building she'd come to think of as her home. Once they turned and were heading down the long drive she continued to stare straight ahead, afraid if she saw Apollo out running, she'd embarrass herself even more by breaking down and crying like the little baby he thought she was.

****

Running had never been to exercise demons, but that's all it was throughout the night.

Apollo finally stopped and allowed his harsh breaths to even out as dawn broke. His mind wasn't any clearer regarding what to do about Isabella than it had been hours before, but he hoped the exhaustion blanketing his body would allow for sleep, if nothing more.

He approached the cabin he'd made into a sanctuary years before, relieved to see Sapphire had used her magic to repair his front door. Unlike the peace he always experience when entering the structure, though still beautiful in its simplicity, now seemed nothing more than a hollowed-out shell, made from the timber of the mountain he loved so much.

Apollo pushed past the living room to his bedroom. He wanted to throw himself on the bed and give up consciousness, but he needed a shower first. He grabbed a pair of boxers from his dresser before remembering he didn't have to cover his body for Isabella's sake. He was all alone again and could run around naked, as he always had.

Before she came into his life.

Though Isabella had been as quiet as a titmouse, not one to fill the air with useless chatter, the silence now seemed so much more prominent just because she was no longer there. It should have irritated, this disturbing of the life he'd once cherished, but all it did was take his sadness up another notch and add to his despair.

His solitude had been self-imposed since he was old enough to leave his parents' home, and he'd liked it just fine. He hadn't been lonely, *ever*. He'd been content. Happy even. Satisfied with the solitary life.

Before Isabella.

Apollo dropped the boxers and went down the steps, before heading to the bathroom. He would clean up and get some sleep, and then find a way to take back that contentment. It was a mistake to have forgotten why he gave up being with a woman. Unlike his parents, and the rest of his family, he knew, as he had for years, he was better off alone.

The shower, as they always tended to do, made him feel better. The magical properties Mother Mountain infused into the liquid running through her veins caressed his strained muscles and hydrated his pores. Ingested, it enhanced the powers to the mystics who lived on the mountain. Swimming, soaking, or bathing in the water invigorated the skin and awakened the soul.

He scrubbed his body down and hung the towel up to dry, snagging another bottle of water to sit at his bedside. The hard pounding at the front door caused him to pause in the process of taking the first step in that direction, and his heart soared. He hurried to let Isabella in, not caring that he was completely exposed. But the face of Nicolae standing on the porch stopped him cold.

Nicolae looked Apollo up and down. "I'm guess you were expecting someone else?"

With hyperspeed, Apollo ran to his room, pulled on his boxers, and was standing before Nicolae again. His cousin's husband grinned, and moved on into the house. "If you *were* expecting a woman, my suggestion would be to slow down once you get her in bed."

Apollo didn't find the joke funny at all. "I'm heading to bed. To *sleep*. What do you need?"

Nicolae pursed his lips. "Somebody is sure cranky."

Since he'd never been so disrespectful to a guest, Apollo backed away and let the man who had become a close friend, in. "Sorry. Bad night. No sleep."

"And woman problems," Nicolae added with a grin.

Nodding, knowing he wasn't going to get to bed until Nicolae had his say, Apollo headed to the couch and plopped down. "Okay, give it to me."

Taking the chair facing the couch, Nicolae looked him over. "Not here to give you anything. Figured you might want to talk. At least that's what Sapphire said I was to say."

A huff of laughter escaped. "My cousin is becoming a busybody."

Nicolae nodded. "She cares deeply where you're concerned. We all do. But I'll head out if you want to be left alone. This way I can at least honestly say I visited, saw you weren't crying all over yourself, and are generally in pretty good shape."

"I don't cry. All over myself or any other way."

Nicolae nodded. "No. You don't let emotion rule you. You never have, according to her."

Apollo frowned, feeling it somehow an insult. "What's the big deal then?"

Shrugging, Nicolae settled back in the chair. "I guess that's what I'm supposed to ask you."

"I don't know what to say to that."

"Me either. Damned women. Sapphire says you need to talk to another man. I got volunteered. You want to go fishing or something instead?"

For the first time since the fiasco of the night before, amusement filled him. "Sure. I doubt I'll get to sleep anyway. The lake?"

Nicolae smiled. "Yeah. You want just me, or the rest of the guys to join us, too? The girls are all having their nails done and stuff. So everyone is free."

Apollo grinned and shrugged. "As long as this isn't some form of Sapphire's version of an intervention, the more the merrier."

"You don't have to say a damned word to anybody if you don't want to. I'm thinking beers, sunburns, and something to fry for dinner tonight is what the day calls for."

Nothing could have sounded better to Apollo. "I'm in."

It took less than two hours to contact everyone, get the boat from his parents' garage, haul it down the mountain to the lake, fill coolers with beer, bait, and baloney, and they were trolling out of the wake and into the deeper waters of Mystic Lake.

The early morning chill was lifting along with the fog, and Apollo was glad he wasn't alone after all. The camaraderie of the men who were both family by birth and marriage was always a pleasure to experience, and behold. They held deep respect and affection for each other as men do, and it was exactly what he needed. There would be no estrogen-driven drama to mess up the day. Which he needed even more.

"It's five o'clock somewhere," Zeus stated, pitching

each man a beer. Nods and laugher about starting to drink so early in the day followed, as well as the sounds of aluminum can tops popping, and finally the increased motor speed when Heracles decided to take them on more than a cruising ride.

Apollo turned his beer up and chugged a good amount down. He knew he should be careful since he'd not slept or eaten since his run, but he didn't care. Today was about fun. And if he got a little buzz going, he wouldn't mind it at all.

Amen-ra fought the wind to move next to him at the bow's railing, where he settled with a nod of greeting. The extra tall cousin-in-law looked like he was quite pleased with life.

"No work, no wife, and no diapers. Thanks for inviting me, man. I needed this."

Surprised, since he'd never once heard Jewell's husband complain about this busy life, Apollo nodded. "No problem. Glad you're here."

"Me too. Nothing like a Saturday with nothing to do but be."

Although he never stuck his nose in anyone else's business, he couldn't ignore being concerned. "Everything okay with you and Jewell?"

Amen-ra nodded. "We're good, I guess."

"You guess?"

With a shrug, Amen-ra glanced back out at the crystal clear vista before them. "Yeah. The babies keep her busy all day, so it isn't like we have much time for each other when I get home from work. But we're okay."

Apollo nodded, not sure what to say. He had no idea what it would be like to have so many small children. Then remembered… "You have date nights? Mom and Dad used to have date nights when we were little. They'd drop us off at one of the other aunt's houses for a few hours, and make time for themselves. The aunts reciprocated as often. I didn't realize it then, but they actually had a schedule to get rid of us for a while." He grinned. "They looked really happy with life when they came back to pick us up."

Amen-ra turned to him, his face filled with excitement. "That's a great idea! Rayne is always saying she and Garrison don't get enough time with the kids!" He shook his head. "I can't thank you enough, man, that's a brilliant idea!" He pulled his cell phone from the little pocket of his swim trunks and punched at the screen before putting it to his ear. "Hey, Rayne," he said, turning to walk off, "what are you and Garrison doing tomorrow evening?"

"What was that about?" Ryan asked, as he took Amen-ra's place. "I haven't seen Amen-ra look that excited since he got ahold of my newest game."

Apollo grinned. "He's just realized he can make time for his wife in spite of having four kids."

Ryan frowned. "Yeah, I'm wondering about that myself. Although at this point, I could use a break."

Apollo took a sip this time before peeking at Dia's husband. "I thought you and Dia were great."

He nodded. "We are… But she's a little crazy right now."

Laughter captured Apollo and wouldn't let go. "Dia has *always* been a little crazy!" He downed the rest of his beer, still trying to get his mirth under control.

Ryan grinned. "Yeah. I know. That's one of the millions of things I love most about her, but it's gotten out of control lately. Her hormones are off the charts. One minute she's high on life and is all over me, and the next she'd crying over every damned television commercial with a puppy in it and tells me I stink." He looked at Apollo with annoyance. "I *don't* stink!"

Since, with the exception of Heracles, Ryan was the best groomed of them all, Apollo was sure he didn't. He couldn't help the laughter in his voice when he said, "Maybe you should use what she uses to bathe. That way you'd smell like her. People don't smell themselves."

Ryan tilted his head. "You know, you might have something there."

About to tell Ryan he'd been joking, Zeus appeared on his other side and handed Apollo another beer. He nodded his thanks and turned back, but Ryan had walked away.

"This is great, isn't it?"

Apollo nodded. "Yeah."

The sound of the motor decreased as the boat slowed, and Heracles yelled down from the upper deck for someone to get ready to drop anchor. When the engine stopped, Apollo lifted the one closest to him, and pitched it out into the water. He heard another splash when Zeus did the same on the other side, and they glanced at each other and smiled.

"Fishing!" Zeus announced, and a small cheer went up from behind them.

Poles and tackle were pulled from beneath the long benches that made up the side seating on the main deck. Bait was pulled from the cooler, along with several more beers, as they all began preparing for what Apollo knew would turn into a big competition.

He and his brothers had grown up trying to outdo each other in every way, and fishing was no exception. Since their cousins had snagged additional men to join in, it only increased the level of fun. Amen-ra was more completion than Ryan had proven to be, although he held his own. Celestia's husband, Sabian, was joining them for the first time. The poor guy had no idea what a ribbing he'd take if he couldn't prove his worth.

He glanced back to see Ryan showing Sabian how to bait his hook and approved the speculative gleam in the other men's eyes. Yes, this was going to be a perfect day.

Chapter Fifteen

Sara wanted to refuse, but she knew it to no avail. She forced herself to sit up before looking at the bowl being held out to her. Her stomach roiling in protest, she took the proffered bowl and spooned a glob of oatmeal into her mouth. She chomped on it with no grace at all, but she didn't feel manners mattered anymore anyway.

The numbness from the shots the doctor gave her had worn off sometime during the night, and now the pain was nearly more than she could bear. She tried to adjust the way she sat, but nothing helped, and her moans only brought her glares.

The big guy who had sent her rapist away the day before was waiting on her now, and he was making his dissatisfaction known. Loudly, and often. Almost immune to his hours of ranting about babysitting at this point, she lifted the spoon and put it to her lips again.

Another entered the door, and she cringed inwardly, certain he was the one who had nearly beaten her to death…however long ago that had been. If he was coming back to finish her off, she would be more grateful than she could say. She chewed slowly, her mouth hurting nearly as much as the other end.

"Boss says they may have a lead. But make sure that one is ready to travel in a couple of days just in case. And I need you to step out of the room. I got something to tell you."

As much as she wanted to die, hearing they may have found Izzy sent her further into despair. She didn't pay much attention to the rest of the heated conversation that followed just outside the door, although she caught that someone important had learned why the other man wasn't the one taking care of her anymore. It was confirmed moments later, when her babysitter returned and instantly crossed the room, to knock the spoon out of her hand.

"You bitch! They've fired my brother!"

Sara shook her head. "I didn't say *anything*!" The last came out on a hysterical sob, as fear swallowed her whole. She couldn't take any more abuse at their hands.

She just couldn't.

Chapter Sixteen

Being pampered like this was, without question, the most wonderful experience of her life. Isabella felt herself drifting off to sleep as the woman massaged shoulders and back, arms and legs, and fingers and toes. The slick oils she used had the most heavenly of smells, and the hour-long session she'd expected to use thinking about her situation with Apollo had been filled with peaceful nothingness instead.

"There you go. I'm going to step out now, and you stay here for as long as you like. When you're ready, put your robe back on, and come on out. The other ladies will join you on the patio for mimosas and a light lunch once everyone else is ready too. Then you will all get manicures and pedicures together."

"Thank you."

"You're welcome," came the reply, before she was left alone.

Isabella sat up, and realized her body felt so loose she had to steady herself to dismount from the table, and lean against its soft mattress while pulling on her rode. Her entire body felt like one big sigh as she made her way to the door. Her masseuse was on the other side waiting and led her to the large room where the late morning sun shone brightly through the glass panels making up the ceiling and exterior wall.

Jewell and Dia were already sitting on one of the two facing couches, and smiled at her as she sat across from them. "I feel like I did after drinking Destiny's wine last night."

The sisters smiled and nodded as if one.

"I know. I haven't felt this relaxed since the babies were born," Jewell stated.

"Me too," Dia added, "Since I found out I was pregnant, that is."

Isabella looked at the ball beneath Dia's robe and then into her eyes. "How does it get out?"

Neither woman responded, only looked at her with unwavering eyes. Light blue eyes turned to the emerald green ones, and Isabella knew her ignorance would never stop being an embarrassment. She shook her head quickly. "Never mind. That was a dumb question."

"What's a dumb question?" Sapphire asked, as she joined them, settling at Isabella's side.

Heat filled her cheeks, as she faced the woman she was coming to know as a friend. "It's nothing. How was your massage?"

Sapphire threw a quick look at her sisters before smiling. "It was great. As always. How was yours?"

"Amazing. I still feel like my arms and legs might just fall off."

Sapphire laughed. "I know. The only thing better than a massage is wild sex." She laughed again. "Though both leave you all slick and in need of a shower."

"Sapphire!"

Isabella turned to Jewell, and knew Sapphire had as well. Jewell sent Isabella a quick glance before shaking her head at her sister.

"Don't do that, please."

All eyes turned to Isabella, making it hard for her to go on, but she knew she had to. "Don't look at each other like that when you're thinking of me. I might be dumb, but I'm not stupid." She held up her hand when all three of them opened their mouths. "I'm not done. I know nothing about anything. I realize that now." She turned to Sapphire. "Before you walked up, I asked Dia how the baby got out. I know I should know, but I don't. I've never been around women with the exception of one, and she, I realize now, taught me very little. I really appreciate everything you all are doing for me. I don't know why you've been so nice to a stranger. But since you are, the thing I really need is information. I don't know about sex. I don't know about babies. And I don't know what I need to do to fix what I broke with Apollo."

Sabia stepped forward with Luna, and looked her man's family over. She smiled at them all. "Sorry, didn't mean to eavesdrop, but I got done with my massage a few minutes ago." She sent Sapphire a cautious look before turning to the others. "Girls, after we get our manis and pedis, I think this calls for an afternoon of wine and porn."

Dia and Jewell's eyebrows shot up, but Sapphire only nodded slowly. "A rough intro into the world of sex, but not a bad idea."

"What's not a bad idea?" Soleli asked as she too joined them."

"Wine and porn," Jewell answered, smiling now.

Soleli looked to each of them, one after another, as Celestia finally appeared. She turned to her white-haired sister and laughed. "Good thing you turned your angel human and not the other way around. These felines have decided we're spending the afternoon watching people have kinky sex."

Celestia looked them over, before her gaze settled on Isabella. She smiled serenely. "Why, I was thinking a Hallmark movie, but in this case, I think graphic reality is the better idea."

Lunch was light and satisfying, the mimosas, of which she had two, divine. The manicure was nice and her fingernails looked so pretty, but the pedicure was wonderful to the extreme. Her feet actually felt *happy*, something she'd never even considered possible.

Isabella watched as the woman used tweezers to put little diamonds on her red painted big toes, declining the option of some on the others. The desire to wiggle them all was stifled by the foam thingies between her toes, which made it ten kinds of awkward for her when she had to walk to the table that then shined blue lights on her feet to dry her toenails.

The uncomfortable discussion of earlier had long since passed, and the women chatted to each other about every subject they could think of. It was so obvious they liked being with each other, although there seemed to be a little tension in the room when Sabia spoke directly to Sapphire. Curious, and deciding they knew all *her* secrets, Isabella turned to Sapphire. "Are you and Sabia angry with each other?"

All the chatter stopped, and Sapphire's cheeks filled with color. Isabella tore her eyes from the surprising reaction and looked at Sabia, only to find regret filling her nearly black eyes.

"I made a mistake with Nicolae once and hurt Sapphire deeply. I'm very sorry for it."

Sapphire sat up straighter, and shook her head. "It's over and done. And I've already accepted your apology." She turned to Isabella. "And we will speak of it no more."

Isabella nodded. "Okay." She bit her lip. "Can I just ask one more thing?"

Sapphire nodded cautiously. "What?"

"If you accepted her apology, why do you still avoid looking directly at her?"

"Isabella?"

She turned to Sabia, only to see the woman was as uncomfortable as Sapphire seemed. "Yes?"

"When a woman loves a man, she can't always forgive

completely, if another woman hurts what's between them in some way. I did that. And I regret it deeply. But Sapphire is entitled to feel as does, for as long as she does."

Sapphire stood and walked over to Sabia, to give her a quick hug. "Thank you, for understanding. I'm trying. I really am."

Sabia's smile stretched nearly across her face, making Isabella realize how contained she'd been before.

"I know. And we'll get there. At least I hope so."

"I do too," Sapphire said, placing a kiss on Sabia's cheek.

Jewell and Luna, then Dia and Celestia stood, and Isabella and Soleli followed. Sandals and flip-flops were placed on several sets of freshly decorated feet, before Sapphire handed an employee a wad of cash. They made their way out to the cars lined up in the parking lot, discussing to which house they would all head.

Sabia invited them all to her place, adding, "Zeus and I have an extensive collection of porn." She shrugged when the others looked at her in surprise or amusement.

The trip back up the mountain was as peaceful as the land itself. Isabella turned to Sapphire, her happiness only marred by thoughts of Apollo.

"Thank you for the morning at the spa. I'll cherish the memory of it forever."

"You can cherish it for a couple of weeks, and then we'll do it all over again."

Although she had no real concept of money or what things cost, Isabella shook her head. "It's too much."

Sapphire smiled Isabella's way, before turning her attention back to the road. "That's something you'll never have to worry about here."

Since she knew nothing she could say would make any difference, Isabella let the subject drop. "I wonder what Apollo is doing."

Sapphire followed the SUV in front of her as it turned into another of the long driveways this family seemed to like. They ended up at another log home, which looked much like the one she'd left just that morning.

"He's with Nicolae and the other guys. They've gone fishing. I'd say by now they're all about three sheets to the wind, and comparing the sizes of their biggest catch. Or their dicks—which are their *penises*. You never know with men."

Since she'd had no idea penises came in sizes, she just nodded about that. "What is three sheets to the wind?"

Sapphire grinned as she pulled in next to Sabia and cut the engine. "It means they will be drunk on beer by now or headed in that direction."

"Oh."

"Don't worry about it. Zeus can drink alcohol until the river runs dry, and he'll never feel it. It doesn't affect him at all. He'll make sure they all get back safely when they're done."

Isabella lit from the car and waited with Sapphire as all the others did, until everyone was accounted for. She followed Sabia into the cabin, stopping short when she saw the décor. Black leather and gold studded thick couches and chairs faced a very large flat screen television set. And, unlike those of the homes she'd previously visited, this one had the oddest objects hanging on all the walls. Black metal sticks with chain connected spiked balls were displayed beside long black braided leader whips and what looked like something to kill a fly. Neon-lit sign figures caused her to tilt her head one way, then the other, before she realized the thin tubing was the figure of a man and a woman, although she wasn't certain exactly what it was they were supposed to be doing.

Sapphire's bark of laughter at her back caused Isabella to look her way, but she was looking at Sabia.

"*Seriously?*"

Sabia grinned. "To each his own."

Sapphire nodded and moved forward, slipping her hand through the crook of Sabia's arm. "You and I are fine. Randy as he is, Nicolae would never go for all this."

Surprise entered Sabia's eyes. "Like I was ever a threat."

They smiled at each other as the rest of the women filed in and looked the room over. There were giggles and gasps, but everyone seemed in fine spirits as bottles of wine were pulled from a refrigerator designed just for them. Isabella decided to just relax and enjoy these newest discoveries. Eventually she'd learn what everything was, but for now, she was just going to have fun, and be one of the girls.

Once everyone settled with a glass in hand, Sabia turned on the television. There were looks exchanged between the women, but this time Isabella felt certain it had to do with the big naked man on the screen, not her. She'd hardly had a chance to see Apollo's, but Sapphire was only partly right. Apparently, like men, penises came in different shapes as well as sizes.

She tried not to let dismay show while watching the man approach an equally naked woman. Then the woman spread her legs open, and everything was displayed, making Isabella cringed.

"Oh my! Is that what *we* look like down there?"

Laugher erupted, but it was as uncomfortable sounding as she felt. As soon as the man stepped between the spread legs, and pushed his penis inside of the woman and started moving his hips back and forth, Celestia jumped up and grabbed the remote control from Sabia's hand to turn it off.

"Okay, mechanics taken care of, how about that Hallmark movie now?"

There were several who quickly agreed, although Soleli

shook her head, and Sabia laughed at them all.

"Hallmark it is then," Sabia said, and nodded to Celestia before the remote was returned. A sweet story about a woman from a different time-period losing her love, only to find another, ensued. They went through trials, misunderstanding, and although they kissed and hug toward the end, there was none of the sex like the first movie.

Isabella sighed with the rest of them when the story ended, and she turned to Sapphire. "They fell in love?"

Sapphire nodded. "Yes. Like the woman on the screen said, sometimes love comes hard and fast, and sometimes it comes more gently. Theirs came gently."

"The first one, the *porn* one…that was the hard and fast way?"

"No, Isabella," Celestia said. "That was raw sex. We only showed you that so you would know how the body joined when a man and a woman had sex."

"*One* of the way's" Sabia interjected.

"The others can wait," Celestia responded quickly, an edge to her voice.

Sabia nodded her head and settled back into her seat with a satisfied smile. "Sure."

Since she wasn't comfortable with what she'd seen, Isabella was more than happy to learn about the other ways another day. She was much more interested in the falling in love part anyway.

"So how do I make Apollo fall in love with me?"

All sets of eyes were on her, but Celestia was the one to speak. "You simply be yourself."

She shook her head. "I was being myself before, but that didn't work! He thinks of me as an ignorant little girl!"

Celestia crossed the room and took Isabella's hand into her own. "You give him a day with our guys and let us catch you up on your education over time. And everything else will fall into place."

A calmness fell over her Isabella couldn't explain. Celestia's word filled her with an assurance that everything she said was absolute truth, and all that was between her and Apollo would actually work out. Isabella nodded, and smiled. "I like the idea of you all teaching me, rather than Apollo. He's already made it clear that isn't what will make him happy."

"Your happiness matters too."

She looked to Jewell, as she'd been the one to speak. "If he's happy, I'll be happy."

Sabia rose and shook her head. "Hold on to that while you can. But don't be surprised when you finally realize you'll be happiest when he's working to make you happy as well."

Isabella didn't understand, but figured she would in time. With so much to learn, she looked at each of her new friends. "Thank you all for everything." She turned to Sapphire. "I think I'm ready to go home now."

Sapphire rose and stretched. "That works for me. Nicolae and the guys will probably call it a day soon, too, if they haven't already. And I'm sure he'll bring home dinner for us."

Isabella shook her head. "That's very nice, but I mean Apollo's and my home. I'd like to go back there, if that's okay with you."

A big smile on her lips, Sapphire nodded. "Of course it is."

****

They stopped at Sapphire's house first to gather Isabella's things, as well as the additional clothing Sapphire had bagged and insisted she take back to Apollo's log cabin. Isabella was glad Nicolae hadn't returned yet, or she would have felt bad about taking Sapphire away. She also hoped that meant Apollo wasn't home yet either. She wanted a chance to think on everything she'd seen and learned while with the women, and to settle herself back into the house she thought of as her own home.

The only way she'd leave it again was if Apollo told her to get out of his life.

It took only a short time to make it back to the house, and she was amazed again at Sapphire's gift when the locked front door was unlocked with a flip of her magical hand. They hugged, and Sapphire showed her how to relock the door, before they bid each other goodbye and then Isabella was alone.

The quiet of the house, after spending the day with such enthusiastic women, was like the difference between daylight and darkness. Instead of the loneliness she'd expected, there was peace, and excitement, and as well. She hurriedly went to Apollo's room and began putting her things away. When she opened the brown bag to pull out the new items, she had to laugh at Sapphire's sense of humor.

The little black lacy thing was clearly meant to entice a man to look upon the woman wearing it. There was no way she would dress herself in such a skimpy scrap of clothing just to work, or hang out around the house. Isabella set it aside, and found another that was barely more, but the material was white this time. Two string hip-holding pairs of panties came next. The white ones all lace at the crotch, the black, with the lace split open.

Isabella dropped them on the bed and covered her mouth as giggles rose up from her gut. She had no idea if she'd ever dare wear the sexy garb, but it was fun to think about it. She bit her bottom lip, and decided she just had to see what she'd look like in something so naughty. She grabbed up the black outfit, and raced to take a shower, wondering if Sabia's number was on the little phone Apollo had given her to use in an emergency, their first morning together. She'd almost forgotten about it. But then, she hadn't had an emergency, until now. And Sabia seemed just the woman to help her solve it.

****

"You sure you're okay?"

Apollo nodded, glad he'd stopped drinking hours before and, even better, had taken a little nap to sleep off the exhaustion from two days and nights with little rest. He'd lost what ended up being a two-day fishing competition—because the others just hadn't wanted it to end—not that he'd cared. The guys had people waiting at home to enjoy their catch, he didn't.

"I think there's music coming from inside your house."

Apollo frowned at Nicolae, and reached to take his fishing gear. "I don't even remember turning it on before we left…."

Nicolae smiled and held the pole and tackle basket out of his reach. "I've got it. You get the door.

Apollo unlocked his door but couldn't make himself push it open. "You want to come in for a while?" he asked, suddenly dreading being alone.

"Not unless you need me to. After I set your stuff inside, I'm heading home. Sapphire will be waiting to see what I caught."

There was no way he'd hold his cousin's husband up, not even when he was wishing he could go home with him, just so he could apologize to Isabella and try to convince her to come back home. After talking to all the guys, and hearing how crazy their women made them — but they couldn't live without them, he knew he wanted to try again. *If* she'd forgive him. But it would have to wait.

Apollo pushed at the door and his mouth dropped open. Isabella was spinning in circles as she danced to the music, wearing little more than her skin. He spun around quickly and took the gear from Nicolae's hands before slamming the door in his face. The sound of deep laughter coming from the other side of the wood barely registered, as he turned again and came face to face with Isabella.

Realizing he was home, the joy of her dance fled from her face, and she looked at him with caution, as she moved over to turn off the music. She set the remote to his sound system down before facing him fully.

"Hi."

Apollo knew there was the slightest bit of an alcoholic buzz still going, or it was that he wasn't fully rested. Either way, he knew he had to be careful. "Hi."

She bit that bottom lip he wanted to suck on, and he was afraid he'd fall on his face, if he didn't find something solid to lean against soon. "You're back."

Isabella nodded slowly. "Is that okay?"

"That's okay… I mean its fine." He shook his head but never allowed his eyes to leave hers. "I mean, I'm glad you're here."

A relieved sigh escaped her, and the movement of her chest drew his eyes. The black material she wore was completely see through, her dark nipples a temptation he knew he'd have to deny himself. For now.

"I thought you'd be back last night, until Sapphire sent me a message on the phone that you guys decided to fish all night… Did you catch any fish?"

"A few. I gave them to Ryan. I didn't know you would be here, or I would have insisted we come back sooner and I would have brought mine home for you."

She smiled. "And did you guys compare sizes?"

"What?"

"The fish you caught. Sapphire said there would be a completion."

"Oh, yeah. Zeus won." He grinned. "But he cheated.

Isabella moved a step closer, and Apollo watched those long legs in motion. When she stopped again, with her feet slightly apart, he glanced up, only to catch his breath again. His eyes zoomed to Isabella's, only see she was amused by his reaction.

"How does one cheat when fishing?" she asked, a little too innocently.

Apollo felt his lips twitch. If he hadn't completely lost his senses, he was certain she was seducing him. He swallowed. "Um... He shot fire out his arm into the water, and several fish floated to the top, already dead."

"Mmmm. That *is* cheating. Did the rest of you *punish* him?"

Apollo's eyebrows shot up. "Uh... No. No one punishes Zeus."

"Except Sabia."

"Huh?"

Isabella laughed and took another step. "Sabia says Zeus likes it when she punishes him."

Apollo knew he should be annoyed at the very least that Zeus's lady was filling Isabella's young head with their kinky ways, but he couldn't get his mind out of his own dick. He grinned, deciding it was time he let go, and see how far she would as well.

"That's interesting."

She nodded, a knowing in her eyes he hadn't expect to see for some time to come. If at all. He licked his parched lips, and waited.

"It is. And a little frightening, too."

For the first time her bravado faltered, and he quickly took a step forward, rushing to assure her. "But not all couples are like them."

Her smile resurfaced, and he exhaled the breath he hadn't known he'd held. "They like to play rough with each other. Some people do, and some people like lovemaking to be more gentle, or a combination of the two...exercising various levels of intensity."

Apollo shook his head, wondering if he was trying to convince her to give him a shot, or if, from her perspective, he was once again being thrown into the role of teacher to student.

"Would you be gentle with me? At least at first?"

Breath swooshed out of him, and he nodded, afraid his mouth hung open again, swearing he'd kill himself if he woke up and was still on the damned boat with a bunch of guys.

She breached the remaining distance separating them and placed her hands upon his shoulders. "Then show me, you're happy, I'm back home."

Chapter Seventeen

"Looks like you're in luck. They can't find the bitch. But they know she's been in Mystic Waters."

Sara had no rejoicing left in her. The mere thought of a long ride to get to the town they'd been talking about would likely kill her before any window of opportunity arose. But she had to hold on to the scrap of hope they held just out of reach. Because her body just refused to give up the ghost and die.

"When do we go?" she asked, knowing questioning anything could result in a slap.

"Doc says you need a few more days, but I don't think the boss is that patient. Day after tomorrow is my best guess."

At least not yet, was all she could grasp. *At least not yet.*

Chapter Eighteen

Isabella closed her eyes, and waited for Apollo's lips to take her own. He complied almost instantly, with a gentleness that erased the last time completely. He took his time and kept the kiss chaste, then lifted his head and looked into her eyes.

"I need to shower."

She grinned at him as her nose wrinkled. "You do kind of stink."

He laughed and nodded. "Yes, I imagine I do."

She sighed when his arms fell away and then took a step back. Now that she had Apollo where Sabia had instructed, they were supposed to be in the bed, and she wasn't supposed to notice she was nearly naked and planning to have sex.

"What's wrong?"

Isabella shrugged and looked away. "Nothing."

"We don't lie to each other."

The reminder forced her to face him again. "I didn't think we'd stop once we got started." She grimaced. "Now I don't know what to do with myself while you shower."

The grin on his face and the step it took for him to get back against her, happened at the same time.

"We can fix that. Shower with me."

She wasn't in need of one, but that didn't matter. "Okay."

Apollo lifted her hand and brought it to his lips, where he placed a small kiss on her knuckles. She smiled in delight and allowed him to lead her to the bathroom.

"Watch me."

The last time he'd stripped in front of her it was in anger, and with a swiftness that left her frightened and denied. Now he undressed slowly as he pulled the T-shirt from his spectacular chest, then untied the strings of his shorts, and allowed them to fall to his feet.

Before she had a chance to feel nerves, he was pulling her nightie over her head. He stopped for a moment and lowered his lips to hers, then sent her panties to the floor as well.

Breathing became a chore when he backed her into the tiled shower stall, which was the most spectacular thing she'd ever seen, short of Apollo himself. He pushed this button and that one, and rain fell on their heads and gently shot at their hips as his lips again sought hers.

Her mind took flight and stars spun in her head, so she could do nothing but hang onto him tightly to keep from floating away. He released her lips and quickly washed his body, giving her a view of each muscle as it flexed at his reach. When he finished, he rinsed quickly and then pulled her to him again, his erection a barrier to her getting any closer than she was.

"I want to taste you. *All* of you."

Isabella nodded slowly, as her body tingled with nerves. Whether from fright or delight, she had no idea. But she suspected both. He started with her lips, and soon covered her entire face. Her neck became a place to nibble, her shoulders a place to scrape with teeth, before little kisses followed and soothed once again.

When Apollo took her pebbled nipple into his mouth, her knees gave, but he held her firmly as he suckled until her body stained to the breaking point and that which was at the apex of her thighs ached with a dull pull never before experienced. He made his way downward, licking the water running over her tummy as he went, and when he spread her legs enough to reach her core, she whimpered and shook at the pleasure of his touch. She felt swollen there, and the dull ache intensified with each stroke. Her body wanted to fold into itself, but she forced herself to remain standing upright and still.

He touched her ever so gently at first, just fingertips exploring the shape and contours of her feminine form. He turned his face upward to look into her eyes, his own filled with pleasure, and she was sure delight.

"I'm going to enter you."

Isabella nodded slowly, remembering the quick and harsh way the man in the porn movie went after the woman, but Apollo took his time, and although it didn't ease that which ached within, it helped to relax. Until that moment, she hadn't realized how tense her body had been.

Apollo pulled his finger out as slowly as it had entered her, and she breathed with little choppy breaths as he glided two back in, spreading her tightness even more. The pressure continually built inside her lower region. He manipulated nerve endings she didn't know existed but was thrilled he had found. The beating of her heart hammered against her chest almost painfully, and the volume of each harsh breath that blasted from her lungs increased with every friction-filled stroke. When he stopped and wedged his chin between her upper thighs she nearly leapt off the floor, as mouth and tongue attacked, tickling and teasing until her little moans of restraint turned up in volume again, matching the intensity of his striking tongue and her now frantically racing heart.

Apollo tightened the grip he had on her buttocks as he stood, swooping her up with him until she was in his arms, and she swiftly anchored herself by hugging his hips with her legs. He held her there, and looked into her eyes.

"Open up for me, *Isss-abella*."

The thickly spoken command took her breath, as did

the slow piercing of his thick penis when he lowered her upon its head. He held her there, his large hands grasping her butt cheeks, and they stared into each other's eyes.

"I can stop now, and we can go to bed, if you want. It may hurt you more this way, the first time."

Isabella slowly shook her head, the pressure so intense she was certain she was about to shatter into shards of exploding glass, afraid she would any second if the climax her new friends told her about didn't happen soon. "I want you now. *Here*. Like this."

The strain in his features eased. He took her lips in a deep and desperate kiss before his hips jerked forward as he dropped her weight mere inches. Isabella tore her lips from his, as she gasped at the sharp pain. He held her immobile until she caught her breath and could turn her face up, to him again.

"I feel all of you inside of me. I think it's too much," she panted, around the pain.

Apollo grinned. "That isn't all of me." His expression changed. "Tell me when you're ready, and I'll give you the good part."

At her hesitant nod, he took her lips again, and rocked his body slowly, and with each long thrust, he went deeper and deeper still. She held on to him, relieved when the pain turned to pleasure, and astounded when her own body began to respond in motion to his.

"Relax. Let me do the work."

She giggled at that and took his lips again, becoming more aggressive with the pressure rebuilding inside. Apollo's gasps into her mouth as his tongue tangled with hers filled her with a power she'd never known nor expected to have. She continued to meet each of his lunges as they increased in speed and filled her so fully she was certain her opening would never survive. Heat flashed over her and then centered at the apex of her thighs where he rammed her tender flesh, while his lips went as wild. She felt his arms go rigid, his body tense, and he groaned loudly as he thrust once more, hard. Finally, that ball of tenseness in her lower abdomen shattered, sending her entire body into vibrating waves of ecstasy, pulling the breath from her lungs and sight from her eyes.

Isabella had to release his lips to cry out at the joy of it, as her body continued to pulsate around his, and then his lips were tearing at hers again, as if he meant to consume her whole. She kissed him back as wildly, unbelieving her energy had only increased. She felt him swell inside of her again, having only just realized she'd been so lost in the wonder of her own body she hadn't paid any attention to his. This time he was rougher, quicker, hungrier, and when he shouted out the second time, she rejoiced as his hot liquid filled her, and she experienced his joy in coupling as well.

Breathlessly he laid his forehead against hers, laughter now on his lip. "Where have you been all my life?"

She reached up and took his face between her palms as he allowed her legs to slide down his, and her feet were again on the tiles. "Waiting," she said softly, her heart so filled with *something* she was certain it must be what everyone called love. "I've been waiting for you, and I'm so happy you finally came."

*****

Apollo pulled the sheet up and tucked Isabella closer to his side. He'd never thought, after living alone for so many years he'd be a spooner, but he couldn't bear the thought of letting her go, not even an inch away.

"Apollo?"

Her sleepily calling his name, made him smile. "I thought you were asleep."

Isabella wiggled back against him, her bare bottom teasing his erection to life. He knew she was already too sore for another round. Although, he promised himself, *next time*, he'd do a better job at retaining control.

"Sapphire said you were in love once before. What was the woman like?"

Knowing he was going to throttle his cousin, Apollo sighed. Isabella wasn't asking out of idle curiosity or jealousy. She was trying to understand the ways of the world, and he wanted to be the one to help her navigate those waters.

"She wasn't a woman. She was a girl. And I was just a boy." He thought back to his father's comments on the subject, but his dad had been wrong…at least in part. "I did love her as much as I understood love at the time. She was beautiful in that way popular girls in school are."

"I've never been to school."

Wincing at his blunder, he sighed again. "Sorry. Let me see if I can explain."

Isabella rolled over to face him, and her nose was inches from his own. He grinned at her, and she grinned back, and he relaxed into the story he was about to tell.

"In high school, which is the ninth grade through the twelfth, here in America, there is a pecking order." At her upraised brow, he shook his head. "Okay, let me explain it like this: some people have power over other people."

"You mean like adults over children?"

"Well, that too, but I mean children over other children."

Her brows knitting, Isabella frowned. "That doesn't sound fair."

He couldn't help but grin. Her innocence was as frightening as it was endearing. "You're right, it isn't. But it's the way of things."

"Okay. Continue."

He chuckled, wondering if she realized she was starting to get a little bossy. "So, the kids who are in charge are called popular, and they pretty much dictate how the other kids are treated."

"So this girl you loved, she was one of the kids in charge." At his nod, she searched his eyes. "And which were you?"

Apollo hesitated, realizing the answer shamed him on some level. "I was one of those kids too."

"Were you ever mean to the kids who weren't popular?"

Apollo was relieved he could shake his head. "No."

"Was she ever mean?"

Knowing he was going to have to get over being embarrassed if he was going to help her understand all this, he nodded. "Sometimes. She liked everyone knowing she had one of the Whitehawk boys wrapped around her little finger."

Isabella grinned. "Unless she was like that giant in the book you gave me to read, I don't think that's possible."

"It's an expression."

She giggled. "I know. I'm just messing with you."

He laughed with her. "And just how do you know this, smarty-pants?"

"I heard one of your cousins use the expression and then had it explained to me."

Since it was a crapshoot to try and figure out which one was the culprit, Apollo let it go. The men in this family were all whipped, if the truth be told, though none of them seemed to mind. "Well, since you understand the expression, you should also understand that I let her use me because I wanted her to like me."

"Because she was beautiful."

"Yes. And because she gave me what every teenage boy wants at that age."

"The sex."

He nodded. "It's not *the* sex though. It's just *sex*."

"Noted. Go on."

Amused and a little bewildered by the need to help her understand the next part, Apollo leaned forward and kissed her lips, to buy himself time, and just because he could.

"Are you trying to get my mind on something else?" she asked, giggling when he nodded.

"But I'll get this over with first.

"I had convinced myself she really did love me, even though my brothers, and cousins, tried to persuade me otherwise."

"They were popular too."

He nodded. "Yes. But how did you know?"

"Because I can see popular people are beautiful to look at, and all of you are."

There was nothing Apollo could think to say to her statement, without sounding foolish. "And we came from a family with unlimited funds... *Money.*"

She frowned for a moment, and then nodded. "So good looks and money make people popular in high school."

She'd nailed it. "In life as an adult as well."

"That still doesn't sound fair."

"It isn't."

"But it's the way of things," Isabella stated with finality.

She was so cute he wanted to kiss her again. But this talk had to happen, so he could be done with it, and kissing, he knew from the urges of his lower body, would only make it harder to get back to the task at hand.

"It is."

"So what happened? Did you finally decide your brothers and cousins were right?"

"I wish."

She pulled herself up and looked down at him, excitement in her eyes. "What did you do?"

Apollo wished he could tell her some wild tale where he came out the hero, but just the opposite was true. "Scarlett was starting to talk about dumping me for an older guy. It hurt my feelings, but worse, it was a big hit to my young ego. I was desperate to keep that from happening. I decided I'd show Scarlett I was *special*. That I had something the scumbag didn't and could do something he couldn't. I took her to a place where we were the only two people around. And I took off running at my hyperspeed."

"And she got scared."

"Freaked out is more like it. She wouldn't even let me take her home. She called her dad and had him come get her. Of course, I couldn't leave Scarlett until I knew someone safe was there to pick her up. By the time her dad got there, she was hysterical. She told him about my ability to run the way I can, and about all the sex she'd had with *the freak*. And then she started saying I'd forced her, because she didn't want her dad's anger directed at her, when he didn't believe what she was saying about my running speed. It ended up being a huge mess."

She looked at him, anger gathering in her eyes. "That little bitch!"

Apollo stared at Isabella for all of three seconds before he pulled her down on top of him and took her lips with all the gratitude her reaction warranted. She was right there with him, the anger she felt on his behalf feeding her hunger for him. He reveled in the glory of her, in the smell of her, in the Viking spirit that was the woman in his arms. She pulled herself up, her lips never leaving his, and she slammed her hips down hard, taking all of him within her.

The bed sheets didn't stand a chance of remaining in place as he rolled them over and began a full on assault of both senses and bodies. He bit her, and she bit back. He consumed her and was consumed with amazing skill for a novice in the art of lovemaking, so when he rolled them again, pulling her back on top, he let her take over, until they were both a panting, slick mess of anger and passion that exploded like the birth of a galaxy, nearly taking them both off the bed.

Apollo couldn't hold her close enough, couldn't kiss her hard enough, and knew he was now completely lost. Everything the other had done to cage his spirit for all these years shattered with this final climax. The freedom of his soul, of his *heart* to love again, was not only restored, but made new as well. Humbled to be given this gift, *this* woman, he gentled the kiss, still paying homage to the one who'd made it all happen.

Several tiny little pecks ended the kiss when Isabella moved enough that his now exhausted penis slid from her.

She lifted her head to look into his eyes. "I think I need another shower."

The deep chuckles that started in his chest climbed up Apollo's throat, and he laughed so hard tears sprang from his eyes. Isabella joined in, and they both had to fight to stop, only to have the laughter start up again.

They finally were able to get up, though he had to steady her when her balance failed. They made it to the bathroom arm in arm, barely releasing each other to wash. Happily exhausted, they remade the bed with fresh sheets, and for the first time Apollo's need for absolute perfection in everything fell with the soiled sheets that hit the floor.

They fell into the freshly made bed together, and he again had to pull her to his side. As sleep overcame him, Apollo knew, *blessedly*, his need for solitude was over and his life would never be the same again.

Chapter Nineteen

Sara walked the length of the room, holding her stomach, and then back, determined to get her limbs functioning again. They'd left her alone, other than shoving in meals, for three entire days. The time was both blessing and curse. It gave her secret time to exercise and stretch a body she hadn't since the first beating. It also allowed her brain to replay all that had brought her to this point, in this journey of horrors.

She worried over the impending trip, and worried more that it might never happen. Their sudden silence, after so many days of questions, had the oddest effect of making her lonely, too. She had prayed for them to leave her alone, but now that they had, it frightened her even more.

She'd needed to go to the bathroom for hours but was terrified because it intensified her agony. That part of her was something she tried to avoid thinking about, but constant awareness of pain wouldn't allow for it. Knowing her bladder and lower intestines were putting up a fight she couldn't ignore much longer, Sara just kept moving, pushing herself, until she had no other choice. She headed to the bathroom, groaned and panted through the deed, and then stumbled her way, sobbing, to the bed again.

Chapter Twenty

Having hot tea, sitting on this magnificent porch, with this amazing man, as the dawn's early light bathed the morning in warmth, was something Isabella had never dreamed a possibility. She lifted the cup to her lips and looked out over the forested land that miraculous was now her home.

For the past few day's one or more of Apollo's cousins had come and spent the day teaching her what they called the abridged version of American history, simple math that she grasped quickly, as well as word usage in sentences which she hoped would make her feel a lot smarter than she felt when talking to them all. Her favorite subject, though, was current events, since she was learning just how big the world was and what went on in all those places outside of the little cabin that was both refuge and home.

Although she hardly thought of it now, the threat of discovery was still on everyone else's mind, so her safe haven was starting to feel a little like a prison at times. After having such a stifled existence her entire life, the realization was starting to press down, hard.

Not that she wanted Apollo to know.

He was wonderful in every way, and she could hardly believe her was hers. He'd given in to her desire to have his cousins' act as her teachers during the day and made himself scarce, going to work with Logan on another log cabin Garrison had designed for Dia and Ryan, since the one they lived in was too small to accommodate their soon to be growing family for much longer. When he returned each evening, she was in his arms instantly, and it seemed established they'd share a wildly passionate time of lovemaking, before he went about teaching her how to help him cook their evening meal.

Dinner was accompanied by sharing their days, laughing over whatever crazy thing either experienced, and following a quick cleanup, they'd be back in each other's arms, whether in the shower, the bed, or whatever surface was handy.

But for these feeling of being *caged* again, her life was perfectly perfect.

"Good morning," Apollo said, as he came through the screened door.

He yawned and stretched, and awareness hit her hard as his finely defined chest and arm muscles did a little dance. She smiled, rose from the chair, and made her way straight into his kiss. "Good morning back."

He kissed the top of her head after anchoring her close to his chest. "What are your plans today?"

She bit her bottom lip, and then released it. "I was hoping Sapphire would take me to town for some shopping."

He allowed her to ease back, and she could see the concern filling his eyes. He hesitated before responding and her hopes for some freedom faded. When Apollo finally nodded slowly, she let the air leave her lungs.

"Can you see if the others can go too? Maybe even the moms?"

Isabella hugged him hard. "Safety in numbers?"

He nodded. "And more power than anyone who would harm you could handle."

She grinned, liking the sound of that. "I'll ask."

He nodded, not returning her smile. "If they're too busy to go, I'll take the day off and take you. I'm just volunteering my time anyway, just to get out of your hair during the day."

Isabella shook her head, not letting him get away with blaming her for something he wanted to do anyway. "You are enjoying yourself too much. If there aren't enough going with me to make you comfortable, it can wait for another day."

Apollo shook his head. "No, it can't. I don't want you to feel like you've exchanged one type of captivity for another. This is your home, Isabella. Nothing less. And nothing more."

Unexpected tears filled her eyes. The generosity of this man never failed to amaze her. She kissed him again, and knew by the subtle difference in his responding kiss, that his held more fear for her, than passion.

"Apollo, don't."

He studied her, his heart in his eyes. "I can't help it."

"If they were close, surely we would have known it by now."

He nodded slowly. "That's what my head tells me too. But I can't chance letting my guard down. If you were taken, and harmed, I couldn't live with myself."

"But for how long do we live with this fear?"

He stared at her, until resignation slumped his shoulders. "I don't know. If you could just remember how you got here, and we could get there, we would end it. One way or another."

"But I can't. Even now, I have no idea how to get anywhere but between this house and your family member's homes that I've visited. I might even be able to get back down the mountain to town, although I'm not sure where things are once I get there."

"If you go, just promise me, you'll make it back to me."

Isabella smiled at him. "Thank you for not saying, 'If I let you go.'"

Apollo slid his fingers into her hair and held her head back as he searched her face. "I don't own you and have no right to dictate what you do. Whatever you decide, and how you decide to handle things, are your decisions to make. Not mine."

"I've never had such freedom. It's wonderful, but it's frightening too."

He nodded. "That's true for us all."

Isabella studied his face and knew peace. "I will be extra careful."

"Have fun as well."

She nodded and pulled him to her, fleetingly wondering if every new kiss of his lips would always feel like the very first time.

****

As it turned out, only a few of Apollo's female family members were able to go. Jewell wanted to, but she'd gotten the babies on a schedule to keep her sanity, and another all-day outing with the girls, since she'd just had one, wasn't in the cards. Dia was having what she called Braxton Hicks labor pains and thought it best to rest at home where Ryan, who worked there on his gaming creations, would be on hand if it turned into anything more. Soleli expressed regret, since she was tied-up at the hospital in town. Only a short distance away, Celestia was busily seeing to her own patients, as her veterinary practice had suddenly taken off after months of her worrying it never would. Sabia had left town in a hurry with Zeus since the man who worked for him found a new nest of demons for them to destroy. And Luna was back in her watery world, and couldn't be reached at all.

Apollo's mother and her sisters, Rayne and Haven, were excited to spend the day with Sapphire and Isabella, and she was equally glad for the opportunity to get to know the former generation better as well. She felt more confident overall since she'd done so well with her studies and because she now knew many of the heart secrets, and about her own sexuality and that of her man's. Of all the things that she'd felt made her different from the rest, those were the ones that mattered most.

For the first time she felt completely at home in their company, so she smiled at Destiny when she held up a pretty cotton dress, similar in cut but much greater in style and design to the one Apollo had destroyed soon after they met.

"Do you like this? I think it would look great on you!"

Isabella nodded and crossed the small downtown shop to take a closer look. "I think it's very pretty. But I really don't need anything, other than time away from the cabin."

"Of course you do, sweetheart! We all need pretty new things every once in a while!"

Knowing she would lose—since she already had when Rayne decided to buy her a pair of pretty sandals in the last store and Sapphire what she called *lingerie every woman must own* at the store before—an argument still fell from Isabella's lips. "This is all too much. It feels so wrong to always be taking, when I have nothing to give back."

Destiny pressed her lips together as her brows did the same. "Isabella, you have given me back the son I bore and raised, but more importantly, you have freed him from a life of self-imposed chains. There is nothing I could buy in a store for you that would equal that in value."

"I just love him," she finally responded, feeling his family was giving her more credit than due.

The delighted smile that lit up Destiny's face was followed by a tight hug that nearly took Isabella's breath. When Destiny stepped back, there were tears in her eyes.

"Have you told him?"

Isabella swallowed, and shook her head. "I think he knows."

Destiny nodded. "I think he does too. But words are important. They hold magic."

Intrigued, Isabella glanced at Rayne and Haven as they moved closer. She turned back to Destiny. "How so?"

The three sisters looked to each other, and then back to Isabella with identical smiles.

Destiny scanned the room, and Isabella followed her gaze to the single clerk manning the store. She turned again, and said very quietly, "You say you have the power to see into the future."

Isabella nodded. "Only sometimes."

"Can you control it?"

Isabella bit her bottom lip. "I don't know. I've only tried it once, and that was with Soleli. I normally only see things when they come to me, but it scares me. I'm usually happy when the visions go away."

"You've probably blocked your abilities then." She glanced at her sisters again, and they nodded as one. Destiny and Rayne reached out to Isabella, as they joined hands with Haven.

Sapphire appeared on the outside of their circle. "I've locked the door and put the clerk into a deep sleep."

Destiny nodded without looking back. She kept her gaze locked on Isabella. "Close your eyes and think of your future with my son."

"How far out?" Haven asked.

"Ah, yes. We should temper it at first. Isabella, look only past today and into the next few days if you can."

Isabella inhaled deeply and exhaled through her lips. She was afraid but excited as well. This was the first time she'd ever been asked to use her curse for her own benefit. She closed her eyes and felt a surge of power coming in through the hands clasping hers. The energy was strong but not overpowering or frightening. She smiled to herself and thought of all Apollo meant to her.

His beautiful face appeared to her, as he looked at her with the same love she held for him. He kissed her gently but with a sob, and then as if pulling on all his strength, with the passion she'd come to cherish. "I will love you into eternity," he said, as a single tear flowed down his face. His head fell forward to hang limply, and Isabella stumbled back, stunned.

Anguish tore through her when she was far enough back to see all of him. His bare stomach was mostly concealed with blood, as a river of it poured from the wound over his heart. She ran forward again, confused but frantic, trying to stop the thick red flow.

Isabella was sure he'd stopped breathing, but his dangling body made it impossible to tell. She tried to hold his head up to blow air into his lips while fumbling to stick her fingers in the hole to stem the blood's pumping flow. But it was impossible to help him, the way he was!

She released him, determined to hurry, as she followed the line of his outstretched arm. She tugged and pulled until her own blood flowed from her fingertips, not caring about the pain, only determined to release the chains anchoring him to the concrete bricked wall. His limp body now hung lower, his bent knees hovering just above the dirty concrete floor. She cried out her anger and grief, and then...

"Isabella!"

Isabella stumbled back, only be caught in Sapphire's arms. Her disbelief and horror were reflected on the faces of the three sisters still holding hands. Destiny released the others and moved closer, their noses only inches apart, her gaze filled with same desolation Isabella felt.

"What the hell was that?" she screamed into Isabella's face.

Her heart in tatters, her body too stunned to move of its own accord, Isabella swallowed the hysteria bubbling up her throat and said the only thing she could. "Apollo will die, if I don't get out of your lives *now!*"

Destiny stepped back, her emerald irises spinning, her face blackening in color, as she lifted up her hand and a ball of blue fire filled it. Isabella scrambled back, but Sapphire was in the way, still holding her up, and she couldn't move. Rayne reached up quickly and grabbed Destiny's arm, her face filled with the panic Isabella suffered.

"Destiny! Stop! *Now!*"

Sapphire jerked Isabella around to her back, blocking her from Destiny's rage. A loud growl and snarling filled the room, as her friend's body began to transform. Isabella stood frozen to the spot, even more stunned as she watched the change from woman to wolf. Haven jumped forward to wrap her arms around Destiny's stiff body, and her hand shot upward too, to keep Destiny from all movement.

Her heart now lodged firmly in her throat, Isabella tried to make out the strange words Rayne said, while she waved her hands in front of her sisters. The words made no sense, but that was likely due to her fear. Sapphire continued to growl threateningly, until the fire disappeared, and more slowly, Destiny's color returned to normal. Everyone breathed a sigh of relief when her body went limp in Haven's arms.

Isabella fell to her knees, unable to take any more.

Rayne wrapped her arms around both of her sisters and turned her head in the direction of her daughter. "Transform, awaken the clerk, and get Isabella back home as quickly as you can."

Sapphire changed and clothed herself as her mother and aunts turned to sparkling mist. Isabella watched, too numb now to react to anything, as the glitter spun until it was a small tornado, and then was instantly gone.

When she turned her attention to Sapphire, the horror and grief of her vision returned. Her face crumped, and the agony tearing through her soul came out of her mouth in wounded wails of denial...that refused to stop.

****

Sapphire stepped from Isabella's room, the surprise at seeing him there in her eyes.

"You're here! Thank God! She's asleep now. I had to give her a little push to knock her out."

Apollo nodded and stopped moving. He looked down, realizing he'd worn out the wood flooring with his pacing since arriving moments before. Ignoring the damage done to his home, he looked at his cousin in anger.

"What the hell happened, Sapphire? This was supposed to be fun for her!"

Sapphire blew out a long breath. "How much do you know?"

"Damned little. Dad called me and said to get home quickly but to let you handle Isabella. So here I am. What the hell is going on?"

She grimaced. "Long version or short version?"

Apollo wanted to hit something, and was glad she was across the room. "I don't care! Just give me *something*!"

She nodded. "You have to calm down first. This is all hard enough to handle without you suddenly becoming...*different*."

He crossed the room and threw himself on the couch. "What does that mean?"

She joined him, a tiny grin on her lips. "You never used to lose your temper."

Apollo made himself relax, one muscle at a time. "Temper contained. Now tell me," he said, keeping his tone even and his words calm.

Sapphire started at the beginning, telling him what a wonderful day they were having, shopping for Isabella, as well as for themselves, since they rarely ever did. Since he knew much of his family able to create their own clothing

152

from magic, he had to keep from grinding his teeth as he waited for her to get to the part he needed to hear. But she was taking too damned long.

"Okay, shopping. Happy women. I got that, move on."

Sapphire licked her lips. "I only told you all that, so you'd know your mom adores Isabella, very much."

Apollo sat up straighter, as anger slammed into his chest. "Did Mom do something to hurt her?"

Sapphire shook her head. "No…not exactly."

"Get to the fucking point!" When Sapphire hesitated, Apollo jumped up, knowing he was going to displace every slab of wood in the living room if she didn't start talking soon."

"Okay… Your mom asked Isabella about her ability to see into the future."

Apollo stopped pacing, his anger increasing. "Why the hell did she do that? I told Isabella she'd never be asked to perform for us, like she was made to do at that place that had her."

Sapphire nodded. "I know, and I wasn't comfortable with it. But it was your mom, and I didn't feel it was my place to say anything, especially since Isabella seemed kind of excited to try it."

Disbelief felt like a slap to his face. "Are you telling me, in the middle of a store, at the heart of town, my mother asked Isabella to try to look into the future?"

She nodded. "We locked the doors and put the only other person in there to sleep."

"Are you all fucking idiots! The stores have large front windows! Anyone could have passed by and looked in!" By the paling of her cheeks, Apollo knew that hadn't been a concern at the time. "Did *everyone* not learn from my disastrous experience all those years ago, how much trouble that can cause?"

Sapphire licked her lips. "No one would have paid any attention to her. She didn't do anything but stand still and think about what's coming."

Relief washed through him. "Thank goodness!"

"Don't get too happy yet."

Apollo look his cousin over, and knew what was coming was big. "Tell me the rest."

Anger, disbelief, and finally rage, overtook Apollo as Sapphire recapped the events of their day. He forced himself to remain silent through the telling, but once she was done, he settled on the couch at her side and put his face in his hands.

"I can't believe my mother would do this to her."

Sapphire reached over and placed her hand on his shoulder. It shamed him that his reaction was to instantly reject the comfort she offered by jerking himself away.

She looked at him, hurt in her eyes. "I'm sorry for this, Apollo. But as much as I hurt for Isabella, I think the bigger issue is what will happen to you. We can't lose you. Not for anyone."

He stood and pulled her up, and wrapped his arms around her. "I'm not going anywhere. If nothing else good came of all this, at least we know it will all come to a head soon."

When Sapphire pulled back with a gasp and denial on her lips, he placed his finger over her mouth. "*Forewarned. We will be forearmed.*"

She studied him and slowly her lips lifted. "We have some planning to do."

Apollo nodded, needing her to get out so he could check on and reassure Isabella. "You round up the troops, and we'll all meet at Mom and Dad's this evening." He blinked away the anger at his mother, still clutching his heart. "But before we call our little meeting together, I need some alone time with my *ma'am*."

"She *reacted*, Apollo! She didn't mean to. It was purely a maternal reaction, because she loves you so much, and the thought of you dying is something she couldn't bear. You can't hate her for this! She's your mother!"

Trying to appease her sudden panic, Apollo nodded. "I know. But she needs to understand. If she ever hurts Isabella, in any way, I'm lost to her forever."

Chapter Twenty-One

Dread and excitement hit Sara at the same time as the three men filed into her room. Two of them she knew on sight, the third, by his dapper dress, she could only surmise meant she was about to meet their ringleader.

He stepped forward and looked her over. "I'm Maximum Barnabas. I'm sorry about what's been done to you by our misguided *former* employee. Contrary to what you must believe, we aren't animals. We are actually a group of people trying to rid the world of the evil that is taking over this country. Of the world, in fact."

Sara nodded slowly, not certain if she was supposed to respond or not. She was at the mercy of them all, and it was clear there was none, even if he was trying to convince her differently.

"I read your file. You've been a good employee the last couple of years. What made you decide to release one of the witches we were holding?"

Sara cleared her throat, knowing not to contradict his assessment of Izzy. "I overheard someone talking about killing her and dissecting her for research. I overreacted I guess, but she's barely more than a child, and I didn't realize her abilities made her a witch."

Maximum nodded, his expression sympathetic. A little *too* sympathetic to be real. Again Sara said nothing. She didn't dare.

"Yes, you did overreact. I'm sure someone was just spouting off about hurting her. Unfortunately, I can't control the way people think or act at times. But, I assure you, if you identify the culprit, they will be dealt with."

Sara looked him square in the eyes, glad her sight was now nearly back to normal. "I didn't see who it was. I just heard them from around a corner down the hall."

One edge of his lips came up in an odd smile, as if he'd suffered a facial stroke and the other side didn't work. The look was probably meant to assure, but just made him look as evil as Sara believed him to be. She made herself take even breaths, but her heart was pounding away inside her chest.

"That's too bad. Do you think you could identify the voice again?"

Sara took a few seconds to answer, hoping she looked as though she were giving it real thought. She shook her head finally, wondering where all this was leading. "No. I can't remember much, since the beatings."

Barnabas studied her, before nodding. "Well, people tend to expose their true selves sooner or later." His odd grin appeared again. "You will be handsomely compensated for all that has been done to you, and your job is secure, if you'd like to join us in ridding the world of its evil occupants."

Not daring to ask what would happen if she refused his offer, if it even *was* an offer, and not a test, she made herself smile, afraid it as stiff and shaky as it felt. "I would like that very much."

Suspicion flattened his gaze. "Why would you do that, after all this," he said, waving his hand over her.

Sara swallowed. "Because I have nowhere else to go and nothing else to do. This place has become my home."

He leaned forward, an evil glint in his eyes. "Are you willing to prove it?"

The shaking started at her core, but Sara nodded anyway. "Yes."

Their leader motioned to the man who had cared for

her following his brother's dismissal, and he stepped forward. Sara eyed him warily, before turning her attention back to the one they *all* feared.

"Dave here has been in want of a wife for a long time, but there are none to be had on the compound. If you agree to marry him, and help us find Isabella Quinn, you will be treated with the utmost respect by everyone who works for me from here on out. You would be well cared for, Sara, for the rest of your life. You will even be allowed to leave the compound with Dave occasionally in the future, once trust has been established."

The thought of any man touching her intimately nearly made Sara vomit, but what choice did she have? "I'm hurt. I couldn't...."

"Dave wouldn't expect you to consummate your marriage until you've healed. He will care for your wounds from now on, until that happens. But once he deems you better, and the doctor has removed your stitches, Dave will expect your obedience and compliance in all matters. As *all* women are to submit to their husbands, don't you agree?"

She wanted to tell them all to go fuck themselves, but there was no doubt she would be slain, instantly. Maximum Barnabas' soft tone, and gentlemanly manners, didn't fool her for a minute. But if she indicated noncompliance, she'd never see the outside of that door again.

Sara nodded, hoping the bile rising in her throat would stay there, at least until they left.

"Excellent," Maximum said, rising to his feet. "The ceremony will be conducted later this evening after our good doctor examines you. And tomorrow, we leave for Mystic Waters."

Chapter Twenty-Two

"I'm not going!" Isabella sobbed. "I'm packing my stuff, and one of you are taking me to the closest bus station! Preferably not *you*!"

Apollo advanced on her, and Isabella fought him, until his hug was so snug she had no choice but to stop. She gave in and wrapped her arms around him, and held on as tightly. But, there was nothing he could say or do now to change her mind.

"Isabella, *baby*, you can't go off on your own! If there is any chance they've already figured out where you are, they'll get to you. Without our protection, they'll kill you!"

She shook her head. "I didn't see my death, Apollo. I saw *yours*! I can't let that happen!"

He pulled her back and grasped her jaw, forcing her to look into his eyes. "I thought you had more faith in me than that."

His words stopped what she was going to say next. "That's not fair."

"I don't give a damn about fair. I give a damn about you, about *us*. Please stop this. Let's get to my mom and dad's, and together we can all come up with a solution."

She wanted to believe him. She wanted it so badly. But the risk was too great. "If they kill you, they'll already have me too. I was in that vision, Apollo. I was right there with you."

Her words put a coldness in his eyes she'd never seen.

"They will never get to you, no matter what happens to me. My family will stop them!"

She jerked her head from his hand. "Your mother was ready to end my life earlier today. I seriously doubt she'll ever chose to protect me over you. And I don't expect her to. In her place, I wouldn't have been stopped if there was a threat to my child or even to the man I love."

He looked at her, his eyes searching and hungry. "Do you love me?"

Isabella knew the best thing she could do for him was deny it, but honesty was their watchword. She nodded slowly. "With every part of me."

He closed his eyes, and bowed his head. When he looked at her again, there was determination in his eyes. "Then trust that I, and mine, can keep us both safe."

Isabella was afraid she'd made a terrible mistake half an hour later when they pulled up to his parents' house. She bit her bottom lip and stared at all the vehicles lined up. It was clear everyone had come to witness what she feared was a showdown between Apollo and his mother. Before he turned off the truck, she reached across the seat and held him in place.

"If your mother wants me to leave, you have to promise me, you'll let me go."

Apollo stared at her. "No."

"Apollo, this is her home. She has that right."

"The only way you go is if I go with you."

The thought of pulling him away from his family, from the land he loved, was too much. "It would destroy us both eventually. I won't be the thing that obliterates your relationship with them." She searched his eyes, desperate to make him understand. "That girl, the one you loved in high school, you mourned not the loss of her, but what you felt you'd done to hurt your parents, your aunts and uncles, your bothers and cousins. I can't be *that* girl, too. I can't live my life with you knowing I destroyed the part of you that makes you who you are!"

He took her hand from his arm, and turned to face her fully. "You are my family now. You are the heart of it. If I lose you, I lose everything."

She shook her head, her heart breaking off a chunk at a time. "No you don't. You are so filled with love and concern for people. You'll find someone else. Someone who poses no threat to any of you. Everything about me threatens everything about you and those you love."

Fury filled his eyes. "There can be no one else! I thought we'd had this all out at the house!"

She nodded, sick to her stomach now. "I know. And I thought I could do it. But look around us. Everyone's car or truck is here. They've all come for you, Apollo. Not for me. For you!"

Apollo flung his door open, but he didn't do as he'd always done. Instead of speeding to her side and opening her door and taking her hand as she stepped from the truck, he stood in front of the vehicle with his back to her.

"Mother! Get out here!"

Isabella opened her door quickly, unable to believe he was calling his mother out. She made it to his side as Destiny stepped outside and moved to the front of the wide porch, followed by his dad and, one by one, the rest of the family.

"Please don't do whatever it is you're about to do."

Apollo looked over at her and then faced his family. Isabella looked up as well, knowing if they hadn't yet hated her after her terrible vision, they all would now.

Destiny looked at her son, and then her attention turned to Isabella.

Isabella took a step forward, ready to beg his mother's forgiveness, only to have Apollo pull her back.

"Yes, my son?"

"Please don't," Isabella said again, more quietly, nearly choking on the tears filling her eyes and blocking her throat.

He turned to her then, his expression one of peace. "Look at that beautiful woman standing up there. Do you see anger?"

Surprised by his soft tone and slight grin, Isabella glanced to his mother, only to find Destiny smiling back with quivering lips, and it seemed a bit of regret and uncertainty in liquid-filled eyes.

"I...I don't understand."

Apollo took her hand and tugged but didn't take more than a step until she moved as well. She walked at his side, confused by his sudden change of disposition. Isabella broke eye contact with him and looked ahead. One face after another watched their approach with concern, but no one seemed angry, although maybe a little apprehensive. She sniffed, and swallowed, as they landed at the base of the steps.

Destiny came down them, stopping in front of Isabella. She held out her hands, and Isabella looked up into her eyes before reaching out as well.

"I'm sorry about earlier, sweetheart. I don't know what came over me. Please, forgive me?"

Isabella nodded, shamed to have brought this strong woman to such a humbled demeanor. "I understand. If I had your power, I probably would have reacted the same way if someone threatened the life of my son."

Destiny shook her head. "No. You wouldn't have. Your spirit is without anger. Your soul is too kind. You have placed the blame for all this on yourself, when you have every right to place it on me. I was wrong. I never asked you if you wanted to try to harness the very real power you hold. And if I hadn't pushed you into it, none of the rest would have occurred.

"Although I am ashamed of my reaction, as well as assuming I had the right to make you test yourself, a greater purpose was served. We now know there is a very real and imminent threat that we are to prepare for."

"It doesn't matter," Isabella insisted. "All that *does* is that I get away from Apollo, and the rest of you, so I don't bring these people here to start with. Then you needn't prepare for anything! Those people held me because of my small power to move objects with my mind. Can you imagine what they would do, if they discovered the amazing abilities of you all?"

Destiny nodded. "We've spent the afternoon researching groups like this. They are dangerous, especially the one we believe you may have come from. The man who owns that one, The Barnabas Group, has several facilities around the country. Maximum Barnabas, it seems, inherited great riches from generations of oil rights and, from our research, seems to have never worked a day in his life. He advertises on Internet sites that claim to have ties with paranormal phenomenon, as they call it. And asserts he has a school for children who have special, unexplainable abilities. But there is an underlying message in those ads. He *pays* people to come to him with their *special* child, which a school would not do. We believe he's hunting for children with powers that defy science and humanity, as most people know it. We suspect he is doing so for some purpose that will benefit him alone."

Isabella shivered, horrified to learn there were more places like the one she'd escaped, and sickened to realize her own parents may have sold her to monsters. She swallowed the sickness clawing at her throat and searched Destiny's face, more afraid for her family than ever before. "Then I must go quickly. The risk to you all is even greater than I knew."

"No!"

Destiny turned to her son when Apollo shouted. She released one of Isabella's hands, to run her palm over his cheek. "No," she agreed with serene calm before she turned back to Isabella. "We protect each other. And we run from nothing."

Isabella's eyes filled. They didn't understand. "I have to. I'm not like the rest of you. You're brave. I'm not. I can't go through what I saw again. I can't be responsible for your son's death... I can't watch him die *a second time*!"

Destiny inhaled deeply. "Then fight for his life. And yours. And all of ours, with us.

"And you're wrong. You are very brave for one so young and inexperienced with life. You got away from them. You drove a great distance until you found us. You've embraced us without blinking an eye. And you are tackling your education head on, at great speed. A lesser person, if they'd even made it here, may have done nothing but tuck tail and hide."

"Those aren't brave things." Isabella said, but she wanted to be convinced. "I just fell in love with you all. With your son. With the magic of your lives."

Destiny's smile was as bright as the sun. "Well, there you go. It takes bravery to hand over your heart to another, because there is nothing more dangerous than falling in love."

Isabella stared into the beautiful emerald eyes, and a peace that made no sense flooded her soul. She nodded, unable to speak, and found herself wrapped in the arms of both mother and son.

****

The large family playroom was packed. The sounds of so many excited voices talking over each other were nearly as overwhelming to Isabella as the purpose of the gathering. She carried the small plate Destiny insisted she take across the long floor, dodging couples or groups, and settled at the far end of the room. Apollo followed with his own plate and took the seat next to her on the long couch.

"Mom wants you to eat something. She seems to think I'm starving you."

His joking tone would normally make her smile, but Isabella was too nervous. "I'm really not hungry."

Apollo shrugged. "Me either, but you can't get together with my family without food being a priority." He grinned. "If nothing else, we won't have to cook later."

Isabella looked into his eyes. Although he was trying to hide it, she could tell he was nervous too. "I'm not going to ask you to let me go again."

His shoulders relaxed instantly. "I'm glad. Because I can't." He looked over the cheese and grapes on his plate and then set the dish on his thigh. "You said something earlier today, and I've been trying to let it go. But…."

Isabella angled her head in his direction, realizing whatever this was, it was really bothering him. "What did I say?"

His shoulders rose and lowered as he took a deep breath. "You said I could find someone else who wasn't a threat to me or my family. I would never, but I guess the question that keeps plaguing me is could *you* see yourself with someone else?"

The question was so ridiculous, so stunning, Isabella almost dropped her plate. She carefully sat it on the small table at her side, and arranged her body so she was facing him fully. "Never. *Ever.*"

A rattled breath escaped him, and she shook her head as she smiled. "I can't believe you'd ever worry over something so obvious."

He studied her face before allowing his gaze to land on her eyes. "I just got to thinking…you're just discovering life. I'm the first man to come into it who isn't a threat to you, and it's natural to feel affection for someone who has become your sense of security. You're still so young. So sheltered against the world by us all.

"My family hasn't been shy about throwing us together as a couple, and I'm afraid you've been swept up into it without even being aware what was happening." He bit his bottom lip, as his brows pulled together. "What if you realize down the road, when all this is over and you are *really* free to go where you want, and to do what you want to do, that I'm not the one for you? That this all happened just because you had no one to compare me, or life for that matter, to?"

Isabella stopped herself from a reply of instant denial. One of the things she'd learned from those present was that nothing was easily dissected, and dispensed with. She let each one of his concerns settle, and gave them the attention they deserved, and then she threw her arms around him and buried her lips against his cheek. When she pulled back, she wasn't smiling. She wanted him to know how deadly serious she was. "I love you. I will always love you. I don't care about the rest of the world. Or what it has to offer. I want only you. And I always will."

When Apollo opened his mouth to speak, she placed her finger against his lips. "I'm not done."

At his nod, she lowered her hand. "I've grown up a lot since you first met me. And I've learned, *from you*, that everything I do is mine to do on purpose. Loving you isn't an accident of fate, or by your family's desire or design. I love you on purpose, Apollo Cavanaugh-Whitehawk, and I'll love you on purpose for the rest of my life."

Isabella glanced around the room, and sighed. "In fact, if we were home right now, I'd be happy to show you just how much."

The last made Apollo laugh, and he ignored the plate falling to the floor as he pulled her into his lap. Isabella was afraid several eyes had turned their way, but she didn't care. She only had eyes for him.

Heracles plopped down next to them with a laugh.

"Mom's gonna skin you for getting food on the floor."

Apollo's gaze never left her own.

"Go away," he said, grinning.

Isabella broke the eye contact and smiled at Apollo's youngest brother. "Clean that mess up, would you? We're busy right now."

The surprise in Heracles eyes was a big as the loud laugher and clapping coming from behind her. Isabella grinned at Apollo. "I think we are becoming a spectacle."

Apollo's sudden grin was accompanied by a raised eyebrow, which he wiggled up and down. "What big words you have, my dear."

Isabella giggled, knowing she'd never be able to think of him as the big, bad, wolf. But she loved the story all the same, since *Little Red Riding Hood* was the first book he'd given her to practice reading. "I've been taught by the best."

His amusement fled, replaced by hope. "Are you sure? About everything? About us?"

She leaned forward and took his lips with her own, uncaring the others were watching, to remind him she was not a child. She deepened the kiss and allowed them both to become aroused, before pulling back. "Keep that thought until we get home," she whispered, and then pulled herself from his lap. She turned to the others, amused by the variety of expression on his family members' faces. "Okay, you guys, let's get this over with. What do we do first?"

****

For the next three hours, Apollo sat back in amazement, watching as Isabella organized his family into groups with a specific mission. Her new confidence was as arousing as it was a miracle to behold. The plans of action, once detailed and refined, were recorded as schedules and assignments by his aunt Rayne. She had the fastest fingers in the family when it came to typing on the computer's keyboard.

By the time assignments were handed out and the meeting adjourned, Apollo was more than ready to take his woman home. They may have all been distracted with the necessity of their gathering, but his mind and body hadn't forgotten her saucy promise, and he couldn't wait to get her alone and into his arms.

Destiny crossed the room from where she'd been in conversation with Isabella and Sapphire and sat down by his side. "She's really something."

Apollo grinned. It took a lot to impress his mother, and few people ever did. "She is."

She didn't look at him, but continued to watch Isabella and Sapphire. "I'm really sorry about earlier today."

He took her hand, drawing her gaze. "Mom, I know you didn't mean for it to happen. It's okay."

She shook her head. "No, it isn't. You're a grown man, and, you asked us not to push her, and still, I did. I was wrong."

Apollo almost laughed. "Can I get that in writing?"

Destiny eyes took on the gleam he and his brothers knew to fear when they were younger.

"Don't push it."

He did laugh then and pulled her to him in a tight side-hug. "All is forgiven."

Destiny kissed his cheek before sitting back up straighter. "I don't want her to know it, but I'm still afraid for you."

"Mom...."

She gasped his hands, hard. "Don't discount any of this. What she can do is real. If she saw your death, and we don't know what led up to it, there's nothing to say all this planning will make any difference."

He nodded, knowing she was right. "I'll be careful."

The distress didn't ease from her eyes. "Mom, don't worry. Nicolae and Sapphire's pack are going to guard us at all times between the cabin and anywhere else here on the mountain. Celestia and Sabian are going to keep their eyes and ears open and make contact with the locals to make sure they're alerted quickly if strangers come to town. Luna and Zeb have the lake area covered, and everyone else is researching and staying alert. No one will get to her, *to us*, without the rest of the family knowing first."

"Just promise me you won't leave her alone, ever. Or be alone yourself."

He nodded. "No problem. I'm not losing her."

Destiny smiled then, although it still seemed strained. Apollo didn't know what more he could offer her in assurance, so he kissed her cheek. "You guys stay in groups as well. If these people come to Mystic Waters, we're all in danger."

Destiny nodded, and they rose when Isabella crossed the room. Apollo watched as his mother and the woman he loved hugged each other before, blessedly, they were finally able to say goodbye.

Chapter Twenty-Three

The doctor's examination was another in a long line of humiliations Sara feared she'd experience for the rest of her life. Maximum wanted to see to what extent she'd been injured while under his *protection*, he'd said, so he was there with the doctor, as was the man she was being forced to marry in a very short time.

Upon on the bed with sheets unchanged since her captivity, Sara was forced to endure the examination and listen as the men discussed her as if she were nothing more than a broken object. Maximum only wanted conformation there were no permanent damages he could be held responsible for—which was ridiculous given the situation, while Dave demanded to know how soon the stitches could be removed so he could *really* make her his wife. By the time it was all done, she couldn't look any of them in the eyes.

Sara knew hate in its rawest form. Every cell in her body was flooded with it, and she didn't know how they couldn't see it leaking from her pores. There was no concern for her from any of these men, although two of the three pretended. They were doing nothing more than getting some sick satisfaction at ogling her. Humiliating her as much as they could was just a bonus.

"Clean her up, and bring her to the chapel."

Sara waited until the others left and Dave told her to sit up, before asking, "There's a chapel?"

He nodded, looking over her still exposed body. Sara was tempted to reach for the panties they'd made her remove but knew it made no difference at this point. Dave would get to look at her nude body anytime he wanted in a very short time.

"To exercise demons when these kids get out of line. Now, take off your shirt and let me tape up your arm. Then get in the shower. I'm not marrying you while you stink."

Sara would have never bathed again if it would keep him from touching her, but she knew he'd haul her in the small bathroom and wash her down himself if she didn't comply. She removed the shirt and endured him rubbing the back of his hand over her breast while he covered her arm in the plastic and taped it down. When he finished, Sara rose from the bed and made her way to the shower with what little dignity she had left.

The water was wonderful, although every part of her still hurt terribly. She was very careful yet trying to be thorough, but in doing so, she was afraid she was taking too much time. Her assessment was confirmed only seconds later.

"Hurry up in there! Mr. Barnabas is waiting!"

Sara winced, knowing Dave's loud booming demands were something else she'd have to learn to endure. She rinsed as quickly as she could, turned off the water, and found Dave taking up all the area in the little room when she pulled back the curtain to grab her towel.

"I got you a wedding dress," he said, holding out a long white gown.

Sara looked from it to him, a scream lodged in her throat. She choked it down, as tears formed in her eyes. She wanted to shout at him this wasn't a really marriage. She wanted to tell him, of all the horrible things they'd done to her, this was the worst. But she took a long breath instead, knowing the misery that was her life had only just begun. She forced a smile, as she snagged her towel to dry off.

"Why, thank you. It's lovely."

The big responding smile and the delight in his eyes weren't meant to be, she was sure, but Sara thought them the most frightening things she'd ever seen.

Chapter Twenty-Four

"Dia just texted me. Ryan has to go to Nashville, Tennessee, and she wondered if I could come spend the day with her."

Apollo turned from the window he'd migrated to several times already today, and shrugged. "Why doesn't she call her mother?"

Isabella wouldn't get annoyed, at least that's what she told herself. He'd been prowling around the house all morning, going from window to window, and it really was starting to grate on her nerves. "Rayne, Haven, and your mom are all involved in something at the top of the mountain. She said she didn't want to bother them."

"We can both go spend the day with her then."

Isabella rose from the couch and moved to him, to encircle him in her arms. "You can't do this. We have no idea when whatever is coming comes, and you need to go on and help the guys get Dia's cabin finished, before you have to go back to work."

Apollo looked at her as if she were crazy.

"I am not leaving your side."

Isabella dropped her hands and stepped back. "Yes, you are. I'll be safe with Dia. The wolves will be there, right outside, and she and I need to get to know each other a little better. We can't do that if you're around. Besides, I've learned from your cousins that time apart makes time together more important for couples."

"Isabella..." He looked at her with exasperation and then defeat, before nodding slowly. "If we do this, you are going to have to promise me you won't leave her cabin for any reason."

Isabella smiled and flung herself in his arms. She kissed him soundly and then wiggled around, enjoying his gasp and the feel of his growing arousal.

"You know, I know what you're doing, don't you?" Apollo asked with a laugh.

Isabella laughed too, loving the *power*, as her lover's cousins called it, she held over him. "And do you object?"

Apollo carried her into their bedroom and stripped the clothes from both their bodies before she could blink. He placed her on the bed as quickly, and for the first time, Isabella got to experience the wild ride of hyperspeed sex, which shook her as hard as him when the climax hit.

Laughing and playing followed and then she forced him from the bed so they could bathe and get ready to go. She'd had to smack his hands away several times to get herself clean without being ravaged again, but they finally managed to get out and get dressed.

Dia and Ryan's cabin was the closest to the mountain's peak, although Isabella now knew there were still several miles to go to make it to the very top. More family property was up there. She hoped to see it all soon, as well as the special place in between Sapphire had told her about, where the mountain's magic was strongest and where Dia believed Apollo's mother and sisters had gone to spend the day.

They pulled into another long driveway, but this time, there were several large wolves stepping out of the tree line to make themselves known. "They are so beautiful," Isabella said, truly intrigued.

Apollo nodded. "They are also very strong, capable of killing any threat if the need arises."

His cold statement caused her to stop sightseeing, and turn his way. "They kill people?"

"Only if there is no other choice."

She pondered that. "How is that explained when someone finds the body?"

He grinned. "The body would never be found."

Isabella knew she should be appalled on some level, but if people were coming to get her and to kill Apollo, she had no problem with them dying instead. She turned back to look out her window and waved to the closest wolf.

Apollo laughed. "Please don't ever stop being you."

She grinned back at him, her love for him taking her breath. "I can't. Thank you for all this."

He turned to her as soon as they stopped in front of Dia's little cabin. It was the smallest she'd seen yet.

"For all what?"

Isabella released her seatbelt, only to find him opening her door. He pulled her into his arms, leaving her feet to dangle off the ground. "For all what?" he repeated.

"For loving me. For wanting me just as I am."

Apollo opened his mouth to respond, but Ryan was calling his name.

"Thank you guys for coming," he said rushing forward, before opening his car's door and placing three thick black cases inside. "Sorry, I've got to go. Running late for a meeting with my board." He grimaced. "They insist I show up at least once every few months. I hate the damned meetings, but I guess I knew what I was getting into when I hired them all to handle the junk I didn't want to."

He looked at Isabella specifically. "Dia's on the warpath. Cleaning the house like it actually has another speck of dust left to conquer. See if you can interest her in resting while you all watch a movie or something. Those babies need to come soon or she's going to end up driving me crazy. She almost ruined one of my computers this morning with dust spray." He ran his fingers through his hair and scrubbed his scalp, his brows pulled tightly together, as he glanced to Apollo. "I guess I have everything… Either way, gotta go, as I said. See you guy later!"

He jumped in his little sports car and backed out, then turned around and took off. Isabella turned back to Apollo, only then realizing she was still dangling in air. "Wow, he makes you look like a turtle."

Apollo laughed and sat her on her feet. "What were we talking about?"

She shrugged. "I honestly don't remember. But I guess I'd better get inside and see if I can corral the cleaning demon."

Apollo kissed her quickly before she headed to the house. She knocked once and then entered, stopping dead when Dia ran up to her with a hard hug. The room smelled lemony fresh, and gleamed like a shiny new penny. When Dia released her and stepped back there was a glorious smile on her lips.

"I'm nesting! Mom said I would, but I didn't believe her because I hate housecleaning! But I am! The babies will come soon!"

****

Isabella was afraid she would fall asleep if the movie didn't end soon. Dia already had an hour and a half before. She moved slowly, hoping her need to stretch and move didn't awaken Apollo's cousin. The woman was carrying quite a load beneath the stretched skin of her belly, and it was clear nothing would do her as much good as a long nap.

But that left Isabella with nothing to do.

She wandered the small cabin, somewhat dismayed to realize the three babies Dia expected would have to live here in this one room until their new cabin was finished. Isabella was just glad she'd insisted Apollo go back to help them out. She had no idea how far along they were on the building, but they would definitely need to finish it soon.

"*Isabella?*"

She turned sharply at the distressed call and rushed to help Dia into a sitting position and then to stand. The water that gushed out from between Dia's legs and hit the shiny floor between her feet caused Isabella to look up at Dia in fear.

"What is that?"

Dia laughed. "My water just broke!" Then she struggled to look over her belly and down at her feet. When she looked up again, there were tears in her eyes. "And I've ruined my clean floor!"

Isabella didn't know what to do. Dia was crying now, so she made her sit back on the couch and helped to arrange the pillows to support her back, before rushing to get a towel. Since the only one visible was the hand towel hanging on the door of the oven, she snagged it, and raced back.

"Don't worry about that," Dia said, and she gasped and grabbed her stomach. "I need Ryan to come back. And I need him to do it now!"

Isabella dropped the towel over the wet spot and searched the back pockets of her jeans for her phone. She'd had it there, she was sure, when she'd left the house, but it wasn't now. She searched the room quickly, her panic mounting with each of Dia's moans. When she couldn't find it anywhere she'd been since entering the cabin, she hurried back and knelt by the couch.

"You phone, Dia! Where is it?"

She winced as she tried to sit up again, then gave up and fell back. "My purse, I think. Or maybe the kitchen? I don't know. I can't ever keep up with the damned thing! Where's yours?"

"I don't know either," Isabella reluctantly admitted. She stood and went to the bedside table to where a small bag sat. She opened it and pilfered, but the only things Dia carried were a wad of cash, lip gloss, store receipts, and her driver's license.

Isabella dropped the purse on the bed and crossed the short distance to the couch. "It's not in your purse. Maybe I dropped mine outside. I'm going to look!"

Dia grimaced and rolled forward. "Hurry," she grunted. "Please!"

Isabella nodded, and hit the door at a run. She made herself slow down as she searched the ground from the porch to where Apollo had held her up at the truck's door. Tears filled her eyes as she made her way back inside. "I don't have it!"

"Take me to the hospital. You can drive, right? Please say you can."

Isabella wanted to refuse. She had so little experience, and Dia was too important to take a chance on. "Let me go outside and see if I can call one of the wolf pack to me."

Dia nodded. "Okay, but they come and go. There's so much mountain to patrol, and most of them are stationed around your cabin right now. If they didn't know you were coming here, they most likely wouldn't have followed.

Dismayed, because they'd been in such a hurry to get over here, Isabella knew Apollo hadn't had a chance to talk to those assigned to guard them. "I saw some when we got here."

Dia moaned and rolled forward again. When she could catch her breath, she nodded. "They're the normal patrol. How long have you been here?"

Isabella thought back. "The movie was an hour and a half long and just ended. And we visited for about a half hour before that, so two hours or so, ago. Why?"

Dia shook her head. "They won't be back here for a couple more hours. We have to get to town. Now!"

Isabella closed her eyes and nodded. This wasn't good. Not at all. She opened them and helped Dia to her feet.

"Can you walk okay?"

"Unless you can carry me, I don't have a choice." Dia looked up once she was standing straight, and her face crumpled. "I'm sorry! You're so nice, and I'm being such a bitch!"

Moments later, Isabella decided she'd take a bitch any day, rather than this terrified, sobbing woman. Getting to Dia's Jeep took great effort on both their parts, and Isabella knew she'd do anything for a shower as soon as Apollo's cousin was being cared for by *anyone* other than herself.

Maneuvering the pregnant woman into the Jeep was even harder, but by the time it was accomplished, Isabella had convinced herself she could handle anything. Until she stepped into the driver's seat.

"It's a stick. You can do this. I'll walk you—aaaah! *Shit*, that hurts—through it. Push in the little pedal closest to your door, and the one in the center. I'll control the stick, when I tell you to, let up off the one in the center, which is the brakes, and then the other one, which is the, fuck! Damn! Sheeeet! *clutch*, very slowly." She panted for a few minutes and then continued. "I'll have it in reverse, so we're going to go backward. But only go back until you think you can turn us around."

Isabella realized her mouth was hanging open, and she snapped it shut. "Isn't it a long way to town? Do you think we can make it before the babies come?"

Dia clutched at her stomach again, leaning forward. The string of curses coming from her mouth this time made the others seem like nothing. She looked over at Isabella, fear in her eyes.

"There's no way. A skilled driver could get down this mountain in forty-five minutes, at best, and that's stretching it. Take me back into the house. You're going to have to help me deliver these babies ourselves."

The trip back in was twice as hard as the trip out, but

Isabella was afraid it was because she was now truly terrified. She didn't know anything about delivering a baby, much less the expected three. The discussion of home births came up after the Hallmark movie at Sabia's cabin. So Isabella knew, the only reason the Cavanaugh women went to the hospital to deliver in the first place was because Haven, the prominent healer of the family, said she'd prefer they use modern medicine so they could appear normal to the other residents of Mystic Waters. She'd told them all she'd only stepped in when there was no other choice.

This was a no other choice situation, for sure.

"Your mother, your aunts... Is there any way you can contact them telepathically?"

Dia grunted through her next contraction and then continued forward, until Isabella got her into the cabin and bed. "No. It isn't my gift. Dammit!"

Isabella prepared herself to do what had to be done. "What do I do first?"

Dia looked her over and shook her head. "My mother and aunts are up the mountain just a little ways. Do you think you can go and get them? I'll tell you exactly what to do."

To go would be to break a promise to Apollo, but to stay could turn a blessed event into a horror if anything happened to Dia or the babies. She nodded slowly. "Are you sure it's okay to leave you?"

Dia's eyes held the same desperate fear Isabella felt, but she nodded and explained how to work the Jeep again, stopping only long enough now and then to curse her way through another contraction. Isabella paid close attention, telling herself she could do it. The only difference between it and the only car she'd ever driven was one small pedal and manually shifting the gears.

Isabella awkwardly hugged Dia as best she could before leaving, hoping she appeared confident. It took more time than she knew she had, but the workings of the Jeep finally started making sense by the time she'd jerked and killed it several times down the long driveway. She sat facing the road after what she feared was half an hour later. Another bout of doubt and nerves hit, but she pushed past them and headed up the mountain toward help.

Traversing the road was smoother than the driveway, but she still had to struggle to figure which gear worked best. Too low and the Jeep threatened to cough itself to death. Too high and it whined angrily and sometimes loudly, depending on the angle of the incline. Concern the vehicle would be destroyed by the time she was through with it, was only outweighed by the urgency of her mission. She kept looking for the markers at the hidden entrance Dia told her about and feared she might have already missed them, because she had no real idea what half a mile was.

The sight of the large car coming her way, as she took yet another of the twisting dips that made up the road, cause Isabella to grasp the steering wheel even harder. She hadn't thought of meeting traffic on the quiet mountainous road, but maybe it was someone who could help. She downshifted, cringing again when the gears ground out their protest, and looked over when the car met hers.

Isabella found it odd the middle-aged man in the back seat looked at her so intently. She nearly ran off the road when a bruised and battered version of Sara's face appeared in front of his in that flash of a second before they sped by. One quick look in the Jeep's rearview mirror showed they'd hit their brakes. Everything within Isabella began shaking, and she struggled to remember what to do next.

The Jeep protested her confusion, shaking and rattling until it stalled one last time and died. To her dismay, it began to roll backward. A quick looked showed her two men had jumped out of the car and were running toward her. She cried out as she hit the brake and tried to restart the engine. Just as it turned over, one of them reached across her and turned it back off.

"Get her, I've got this!"

The one that spoke jumped in on the passenger side and rammed the gear into first. The scream of the gear box was lost to her as her own screams preceded the needle being plunged into her neck.

Chapter Twenty-Five

Sara held the unconscious Izzy against her, horrified that all she'd suffered had been in vain. They hadn't even made it to the town of Mystic Waters and now were heading back to the compound, so her hope for escape was lost as well.

She wanted to hate Izzy. She wanted to blame every miserable minute she'd endured on the girl. But she couldn't. Izzy was nothing more than another hapless victim of these horrible men. And, Sara knew, at the end of the long drive Izzy was destined to become their science experiment again. Dead or alive.

Chapter Twenty-Six

"I hope you're wrong."

Apollo glanced over at his older brother, before turning his eyes back on the ribbon of road. "Me too. But the feeling is too strong. I just need to check in on them, and then we can go back and finish out the day.

"Thanks, by the way, for coming back home. I know you have demons to destroy."

Zeus shrugged. "We were able to take care of the small den Craven stumbled across, quickly. And there will always be more, unfortunately. But saving the world can wait, until we know everyone here is safe."

Apollo knew he was being ridiculous. At least he prayed he was. He'd fought feeling Isabella was in trouble for as long as he could, before sharing his concerns with those who had gathered to get Dia's house finished before her babies came.

It was a relief to pull into her driveway but irritating when he saw Dia's Jeep gone. He glanced at Zeus and rolled his eyes. "I told Isabella not to go anywhere!"

His brother smiled. "Yeah, how's that working out for you?"

Apollo laughed, relieved to know his little minx had a mind of her own. He stopped in front of the cabin and threw it in reverse.

"What was *that*?" Zeus asked quickly, but he was out the door before Apollo heard the muffled scream himself.

He threw the truck into gear and shut the motor down, making it to the door before Zeus. Apollo threw it open, looked around, confused. A gasp drew his attention, and he made his way to the bed. Dia was curled up in as tight a ball as her huge stomach allowed for, trying to deliver a baby herself. Zeus pushed him to the side and wrestled the newborn from her bloody hands.

"Where's Isabella!"

Dia fell back, her eyes glazed over, and he hurried to push her sweaty hair from her face. His concern for his cousin was tearing at him, but not seeing Isabella, knowing the Jeep was gone, turned his stomach upside-down.

"Dia, honey, look at me."

Her blue irises had turned into a kaleidoscope of pastel colors, as they always did when her magic was in full force. He licked his lips, trying to remain calm. "Dia, where is Isabella?"

She curled up with a sharp cry and screamed, "Went to get *help!*"

Zeus handed him the first child and went back to help the one just crowning, determined to make its way into the world. Apollo turned left, then right, looking for a place to lay the child, and nearly cried out his relief as blue sparkles flowed into the room. Suddenly Rayne was standing by his side.

"Give me the child."

Apollo did so quickly, but there was no relief to be had. "Isabella's gone!"

Her face paled. "Go! Dia's Jeep is sitting in a ditch up the mountain, and no one was in it!

"Zeus, go with him! I've got this. My sisters will be here within seconds."

He nodded but had no time to wait as Zeus was pulling the second child from between their cousin's legs. He was in the truck and pulling it around as Zeus came running. He caught the handle of the door and pulled himself up as Apollo floored the gas pedal, and the door slammed shut.

"Shit, bro! You nearly fucking killed me!"

Apollo looked over but didn't say a word. He had no idea where to look for Isabella, but he was certain, from their talks, she'd come from somewhere to the west. He shot up the mountain as quickly as the truck safely would, only that slowly because he would do her no good dead. Twists and turns caused his tires to squeal and brought additional curses from his passenger, but Apollo had no thought for anything, except to find the woman he loved.

Chapter Twenty-Seven

Isabella opened her eyes, but it took a few moments for reality to set in. Her head was fuzzy, her mouth dry, and, as she looked at the back of the heads of the men in the front seat, her stomach rolled.

"Izzy," a familiar voice whispered in her ear. "Close your eyes. Don't let them know you're awake."

She closed her eyes quickly, relieved, at least, that Sara was with her.

A man's voice right next to her other ear, asked, "What did you say?"

"I was just wondering how much farther. I need to go to the bathroom, Mr. Barnabas."

"A few more hours," was the reply.

Isabella forced herself to relax, allowing her head to loll in whatever direction it would when they hit pothole or ditch or whatever was making the car such a rough ride.

She waited, hoping Sara could convince them to stop.

"It's been too long since we left this morning. I really need to go bad."

Good, Sara! Get them to stop!

Isabella felt the movement of the man next to her.

"Find us someplace decent, and we can all take a break."

"Yes sir, Mr. Barnabas!"

Isabella waited a few minutes then dared to open her eyes just enough to bring light into them. She was relieved she was lying against Sara's shoulder, and that her head was turned away from the man who had made it his mission to destroy lives.

The light helped clear up lingering fuzziness in her brain, but she was afraid to push her luck. Whatever it was they shot into her neck wasn't something she wanted to experience again. She closed her eyes when a hard bump threw her head up and over, but now she was hanging forward, with only the seatbelt holding her in place.

To her relief, she felt the car turn to the right, and was certain they'd taken an exit ramp. The squeezing of her hand, on Sara's side, was confirmation they were about to stop.

She was thrown forward again then the engine was cut. Isabella hung there, waiting, to see how they would retain control.

"I'm hitting the men's room. Sara, you go with Dave. He'll not leave your side, so don't try anything stupid. Sam, you watch this one until we get back."

"Yes, sir."

"May I lay Izzy back? She looks like she's choking."

Thank you, Sara!

"Sure, get her settled."

"Sam," he said a few seconds later. "Prepare another shot. I don't want her waking up while we're on the road. No telling what kind of magic she's learned she's capable of since leaving us, and I don't want to find out she can flip the car or something equally disastrous until we get her back in her cage."

"Yes sir, Mr. Barnabas."

Flip the car? Can I? Excitement filled Isabella as they all exited the car, but her relief tempered with the reality that if she escaped now, the bruised and battered Sara would still be in their clutches. At the sound and feel of the trunk popping open behind her, Isabella struggled with what to do, but there was no time to worry it out. She undid the seatbelt and opened her eyes enough to get her bearings.

Sara was being dragged toward the minimart-gas station doors, her eyes widening at what she saw Isabella doing. Isabella smiled at her and nodded.

Sara turned forward quickly when the man controlling her looked back at the car. She leaned into him and kissed him, before he placed an arm around her shoulders and pulled her to him hard. Isabella felt sick, wondering just what all Sara had endured on her behalf.

"Oh, *shit!*"

The driver, with needle in hand, opened the back door quickly and jumped inside as Isabella scooted back. He lunged at her, and she caught his arm, determined to keep the syringe from breaking her skin. They struggled, him grabbing at her with one hand, the other swinging wildly as he tried to stick her with the needle, and her using all the might she possessed to keep either from stopping her escape.

It took only seconds for Isabella to know she couldn't hold him off for much longer, so she focused and envisioned his arm bending at the elbow. When it did, he grunted, and swore, and did again when she pictured his hand bowing at the wrist as the needle inched closer to his throat. Isabella kept her hand clamped on his arm as a safety precaution but no longer had to worry about his free hand as he was using it now to try and pry the other away. She took a second to enjoy the fear in his wide eyes, hoping he now knew what she'd felt. Seeing he was about to scream, she closed his throat with a thought, strangling his ability to breathe. With one last hard push of her mind, Isabella sent the needle into his neck and made him push the plunger home.

He dropped instantly.

She turned around, ready to grab the door handle and flee, but the barrel of a gun was pointed directly at her face from outside the open window, and Maximum Barnabas was smiling with delight.

"I knew you had powers, but that was magnificent!" He didn't even glance away as he instructed, "Dave, get us another shot for our friend here. And don't worry about what she can do. If she tries to stop you from giving it to her, I'll blow her fucking head off."

Isabella wanted to make him point the gun at himself, but as had happened in all the years they'd made her perform like a circus act, her energy was immediately spent after only one show. Refusing to cry, at least outwardly, she thought of Apollo, of the life she'd suddenly lost, of the love she was determined to keep with her until they killed her and cut her apart.

Grateful he wasn't with her, and out of their reach, she lifted her eyes to Maximum Barnabas's face to stare at him with all the hatred blooming in her heart, only wincing when the needle entered her skin and the burn began.

Chapter Twenty-Eight

Apollo pulled off the interstate at the occasional exit at Zeus's urging, and the frustration of no one having seen Isabella in a car at the closest gas stations along the strip was beginning to take its toll. They were wasting time, and he swore to himself, this one would be the last.

He turned off the truck and slammed his door behind him as he headed to the entrance. Zeus hurried in the opposite direct to stop at the edge of the building. "Bro!" he shouted. "Come here and look!"

Apollo hurried over and glanced to where he pointed. Just visible, at the back of the building, two police cars, their blue lights flashing, sat next to an ambulance with its back doors hanging open. He hurried their way, not daring to go in what was now his usual fashion, but he was still able to catch the last words coming from the beefy man sitting on the floor of the ambulance.

"I'm not drunk! I told you, that witch made me stick the needle in my neck!

Excitement filled him, but Apollo made himself look disgusted as he approached. He turned to the closest office. "I see my uncle has been at it again." He reached out his hand, and received a firm shake in return.

"You know this man?" Office Johnson, *according to his badge*, asked the sleazebag.

He shook his head, eyeing Apollo warily, and Zeus even more so when he stopped at Apollo's side.

Zeus nodded to the officer, and Apollo could tell the much bulkier version of himself made both this law enforcement professional, and the one approaching from the other car, a little nervous.

As they should be.

Apollo grinned. There was nothing like carrying a lethal weapon at one's side. Or at least walking beside it.

For the officers' benefit, he took on a look of patient resignation and longsuffering. "My aunt's been worried sick for hours. Uncle Jason has Alzheimer's and is constantly running off and getting lost, and he's delusional as well. Poor old guy is always claiming some witch or the devil himself is after him these days. *This time*, he's gotten a lot farther than before, and we're all afraid might become violent again. That's why she sent the two of us. We're the only ones who can handle him, but she's going to have to give it up and put him in a home soon. I've got better things to do with my time."

"That's a fucking lie!"

Zeus stepped forward, and the second office stepped up to intercept him, then seemed to think better of it when Zeus look down his nose at him. He nodded once, stepped back, and Zeus continued on, until he stopped in front of their new uncle.

"Come on, Uncle Jason. Aunt Lil is going to be so happy to see you."

"Looks like you guys can take it from here. But next time have her call us. That's what we're here for."

"We should get their information and file a report."

Officer Johnson nodded. "You go ahead. I'm off-duty. I just stopped because you were already here."

The other took on a look of intense aggravation. "I'm off now, too." He eyed Zeus and their alleged uncle. "Next time, call the station and someone will take care of this for you."

Zeus grinned one of his scary grins, and pulled their newly ordained uncle out of the ambulance and let the emergency technician close the doors. He held Uncle Jason tightly, as the enraged man yelled and screamed for the officers to take him with them. But they just send Apollo a sympathetic look, before getting in their cars and turning off their lights.

"Let's get this piece of shit out of here before they change their minds," Apollo said between clenched teeth, sidling up to Zeus. He took their prisoner's other arm, as Zeus leaned over his shoulder and threatened to shut him up permanently if he made another sound. That bit annoyance taken care of, they dragged the now quiet man back to the truck. Apollo reached inside and pulled out the small ball of string he'd pitched in there earlier in the day. The leveling yarn came in just as handy as a wrist restraint as it did to align roofing, when lassoed around wrists enough times to give it strength.

With their new uncle's arms securely tied behind his back, they shoved him into the cab of the truck, and Apollo slowly made his way out to the highway.

"Why did you do that?" their passenger finally found the nerve to ask. "I ain't your damned uncle Jason!"

Apollo threw Sam an annoyed glance, and then looked around him to Zeus. His brother lifted his arm immediately and placed it across the back of the seat. Smiling, satisfied Zeus was in tune with his needs if the creep didn't cooperate, Apollo began what he hoped would be a short and productive investigation. "Who are you?"

"Sam. Sam Benton. What's it to you?"

Apollo stared straight ahead, weaving in and out of traffic. "Well, Sam, it's like this. You, and others, made a terrible mistake. You took my girlfriend, and I want her back.

The man at his side got very still. "I don't know what you're talking about."

"Wrong answer," Zeus said, and a flash of light flashed

in the cab.

Apollo braced himself and tried to concentrate on the road as Sam's furious scream of pain nearly split his eardrum. He glanced over at his brother behind their passenger's back, since Sam was bent forward in the seat. "He screams like that again, burn one of his eyes out."

"Will do," Zeus responded, a grin on his lips.

"I'll talk! Shit! What did you do? You got a fucking cattle prod back there?"

"Something like that. Now sit back and get cooperative, or your days only going to get worse," Zeus assured him. "Who took Isabella Quinn?"

Sam cautiously sat up straighter, and finally rested his back against his arms and the seat. "I didn't take her. I just drove for the guy! Maximum Barnabas has the fucking witch!"

Apollo listened with satisfaction at the second scream, although this time Zeus must have exercised a little restraint. It wasn't quite as loud.

Apollo had expected the answer, but having the Barnabas name confirmed made his stomach flop and *then* flip.

The more research his family had done on the man himself, the more that bastard's subterfuge surfaced. With generations of family wealth at his disposal, the creep had inherited a spot as chairman, or some other high-ranking board member position, on several children's charities upon his father's death. From organizations providing meals for families with small children to hospitals specifically serving the medical needs of the young, the Barnabas name held weight in the world of philanthropist.

Unlike his father, Maximum hadn't had to work for any of it.

He owned several housing developments, *inherited also*, catering to those needing government funding to survive, but reports surfaced repeatedly that those places were often unfit for habitation. He'd been married three times, but all three of those women went completely off the radar after filing police reports against him, until there was an obscure obituary—sometimes months, sometimes years—later. News agencies speculated about him but never more than once. The wives' families made claims of terror and abuse that were quickly hushed up. Law enforcement agencies investigated, but there was nothing to indicate charges were to be leveled against him. Then his face would show up in photographs with high-level government officials at one function or another.

From all Apollo's family gathered, it was clear the man used his name to cover up his dirty work and keep himself out of trouble with the law.

"Where are they headed?" Apollo asked, not caring that his voice reflected the anger brewing at the center of his gut. Rayne had located three possible towns within a five hundred mile radius on the Internet ads she'd found, but there was never any indication of an exact location in those towns where his *schools for the gifted* were located.

"Sakadia Springs, Arkansas."

The closest! "Give me an address."

Sam took a deep breath. "Look, you could have only just met Izzy. You don't have any idea what she's capable of. She's dangerous! She made me stick myself with a knockout injection. She can move things around with her mind and takes away the control others have over their own bodies. You should thank us for coming to get her!"

The rage filling him was barely contained as he asked, "*Why* would she have done that?"

Sam's hesitation was telling, as was the fear when he turned to look Apollo in the eyes.

"Because I was trying to give it to her, so we could make it back to the institute safely."

He cursed as Sam's screams nearly caused Apollo distraction enough to hit the car he'd flown up to, but he swerved, took the next lane, and pressed down on the pedal harder. When Sam got his breath back, he look from Zeus to Apollo and back to Zeus again, his eyes so wide they bugged out.

"What the hell are you? You're one of them witches!"

"If anything happens to Isabella Quinn, we're your worst nightmare," Apollo offered with dead calm.

Chapter Twenty-Nine

Sara backed away from her husband, her gaze glued to the leather belt in his hand. She made herself stop, to stand completely still, knowing there was no way out.

Satisfaction settled in Dave's cold eyes, and his thick lips lifted in triumph. "Take off your clothes and bend over."

Sara swallowed and began unbuttoning the summer dress, unable to believe the second they'd dropped off Maximum Barnabas and Izzy, and they'd made it to his shabby little house, she was to be whipped. "I don't know what I did."

"You knew that bitch was awake when we stopped. It's why you insisted you had to go to the bathroom."

Fear that they'd discovered her deception made her fingers tremble even harder. "I really had to go! You know that! You were right there watching me pee!"

She flinched when he took an aggressive step forward. But he stopped, allowing her to continue to disrobe.

"Don't sass me, woman. Do as you're told!"

Sara hated the tears forming in her eyes, knowing any sign of weakness would only feed his need to dominate with brutality. She dropped the dress to the floor and forced herself to look back up. "I'm sorry. I didn't know what to do. She was awake, and I was afraid if I said anything, she'd hurt me," Sara lied.

Surprisingly, he nodded slowly, his brows furrowed.

"Yeah, after what she did to Sam, I can see that happening."

Everything within her relaxed in relief, until he eyed the belt, and the gleam reentered his eyes.

"But you need to be an obedient wife, no matter what. Drop your panties, and bend over."

Sara stood frozen. She couldn't make herself move. Her body was a mass of sores. With the stitches still in place, her ability to use the bathroom each time was such a horrible ordeal she was getting what she feared was an infection. She had to try to appeal to him one last time. "Please. I'm still healing! Mr. Barnabas said you'd let me heal!"

Unease replaced determination in those cold eyes, and Sara prayed his fear of his boss was greater than the brutality that made him into the monster he was. But then he smiled, and her stomach sunk again.

"Mr. Barnabas is the one who wants you punished for your disobedience. Now bend over, or I'll chain you to that wall in the basement, and this belt won't be the only thing you'll feel."

Chapter Thirty

Isabella opened her eyes slowly, only to see the bubbly white ceiling, which still held pencils sticking out, from when she'd gotten angry in one of the session years before. She closed her eyes again, unable to believe all that came rushing back.

Oh, God! I'm here!

They'd brought her back to the now thinly disguised prison she'd spent her days in when they'd wanted her to perform, instead of the small house she and Sara had shared. She took a moment to process the odd things she felt holding her neck, arms, and wrists, and then realized she was strapped down and held immobile from head to ankles.

Afraid she was being watched, Isabella didn't fight the restraints. Her mind was too muddled to concentrate enough on making them unfasten anyway, and even if she could, there was likely someone just out of her line of vision waiting to inject her again. She couldn't let that happen, or all hope was lost.

The first thing she had to do was find a way to clear the drug's effects from her mind. Which meant time. But she couldn't just lie there and wait. She needed to think! To plan. To find a way out of all of this.

But it was too much to process at once!

Deciding on the one thing that might help, she turned her thoughts to more pleasant things: Of her time away. Of the days and nights with Apollo. Of the wonderful family that had taken her under their wings. The hardest to revisit was the love that had bloomed over those precious few days, and nearly choked her now to remember.

She pushed the pain of loss away, unable to bear it, and let her mind wander back to her first memories of herself as a child. She'd always felt a little lost, even though she'd never known or understood that the men taking care of her followed by the isolation with Sara, made her life different than that of any normal child. She had no memories of a mother, or a father, and wondered if she'd somehow frightened them into selling her to Maximus Barnabas as an infant.

Had she been able to move objects from the start? Had she done something to hurt them, without even knowing it? Though it made no difference now, if she *was* to put to death, she really wanted to know the answers first.

"I see you've awakened, my dear."

Isabella's breath rattled in her chest. For the split-second it took to be denied the ability to turn her head, she'd forgotten about the brace holding her neck and head in place.

"As you can see, we've learned to be more careful with you."

His face suddenly appeared over top of her, giving her a distorted view of his features as the nostrils of his nose and under-chin came into view. When he lowered his head to look down at her, the kindness in his brown belied the upturn of one side of his lips.

"You have nothing to say?"

She didn't. And wouldn't. Give him the satisfaction.

"You will, you know. Once I send my men in here. If you don't answer the questions I have, you'll feel the brunt of my anger.

A vision of Sara's face, and the stiff way she'd walked outside of the car on their trip here, filled Isabella's mind. They'd hurt her badly.

"Sara?"

He nodded. "Yes, Sara was a little reluctant to offer up information and you see what happened to her."

Isabella nodded, as much as the restraint allowed.

"I had you examined when we got here. It looks like you've had quite a few new experiences since you left us."

Not comprehending, Isabella just stared up at him.

He grinned, showing perfectly white, straight teeth, before he leaned to the side, and she felt his hand between her legs. Outrage clashed with the realization that his skin had touched her pubic area directly. Tears filled her eyes, and she attempted to buck her lower body to make him move away from her nude form, but she could barely move at all.

"Now, now," Maximum chided, again standing over her. "There's no reason to act all enraged. It isn't like when you were here before. You were all that was innocence, and I'd never let anyone touch you. But now you've gone and whored yourself out for a stranger, or *strangers*, so, surely you don't mind doing the same for some of my men. They rarely get a chance to take care of that little issue."

His grin was evil itself. "Of course, they'll have to knock you out again first."

Anger as she'd never experienced, overcame Isabella and she balled her hands into fists.

Maximum reached beside her head and lifted a syringe, holding it over her so she could see that he was capable and ready to inject her again. She tried to shake her head, and more tears of frustration poured out of her eyes. She didn't want them to have access to her...to do *hideous things* to her, even without her knowledge.

Isabella forced herself to calm down. "Please. Don't. I'll be still."

"Ah. Now that's a good girl. You see, you give yourself away. It's your eyes. They spin and take on an altered color when your wickedness is building. So be warned, if you try to use your voodoo on anyone here, you'll not only get knocked out, you'll be sorely abused while you are." A short huff of laughter escaped him. "Although I prefer to think of it as being punished.

"Do you *want* to be punished?"

Knowing she had no choice but to talk to him, she responded, "No."

"Are you going to behave, and do everything I and the others ask of you?"

Isabella nearly choked, but was finally able to respond, "Yes."

"Am I going to have any more trouble out of you?"

"No."

"No, what?"

Isabella stared straight up at him and knew her life was truly over. "No, sir."

He tilted his head and smiled down at her as if she were a beloved child. "Now that's my good girl."

Chapter Thirty-One

"Military installations don't have this kind of security." Zeus grumbled. "This place is a freakin' fortress."

Apollo nodded, and glanced at Sam. They'd bound his feet so he couldn't take more than a foot's step at a time, and had covered his mouth with the thick material infused tape Apollo kept in his truck all the time, in addition to Sam's arms staying soundly bound. The piece of shit looked exactly like what he was. A prisoner whose life hung precariously in the balance. And as far as Apollo was concerned, letting him live could go either way.

He tore the tape off the man's mouth and clamped his hand over the scream that would have followed. "You make a peep louder than a whisper, and my brother is going to burn your balls right off of you. Got it?"

Sam nodded quickly, and Apollo lowered his hand. "How do we get in here without being seen?"

"There isn't a way if the guards are still patrolling."

Apollo reared back to punch his jaw, but Sam threw in quickly, "I'm not lying! If there was another way in, I'd tell you! I'm on your side now. I'll help any way I can, if you promise, when you have her, you'll let me go."

"He's telling the truth, bro. We're going to have to do this the hard way, or just say fuck it, and let me burn everything and everyone inside to ashes until we reach her."

Apollo's mind was on Isabella, and getting to her as quickly as possible. For possibly the first time in his life, he didn't catch Zeus's unsaid meaning. "What hard way?"

Zeus sighed. "Get you head together. We can't do this

if you don't. Those guys will shoot us on site if they think we pose a threat." He glanced over to Sam, and got a nod. He looked at Apollo again, and shook his head. "The front gate."

"How the hell are we going to get in through the front gate?"

"I can help!"

"Quiet down, you idiot!" Apollo nearly punched Sam again, but he knew Zeus was right. He had to calm down and get his thoughts in gear. Otherwise, Isabella would be lost to him forever. He took a long, drawn-out breath and leveled his gaze on Sam. "How can you help?"

The look Sam passed between Apollo and Zeus was a mixture of nervous excitement and absolute fear, especially when his gaze landed on Zeus. He swallowed, half turned, and stuck his rump out at Apollo.

"I've got a small ring of keys to the gate in my rear pocket. I was Mr. Barnabas's driver, so I had to open and close the gates without setting off the alarm."

Apollo glared at him. "Why the hell didn't you say so?" he whispered, harshly. "We've been looking at fifteen feet of electrified razor wires for the past half hour!"

Sam glanced back. "You had my mouth taped."

Zeus sent Apollo an amused look. He didn't send one back. Instead, he lifted Sam's suit jacket and pulled the keys out, before making a B-line to the series of locks that controlled the entrance to the compound.

"Wait!" Sam whispered, loudly. "If you don't do the locks in the right order, the alarm will squeal like a stuck pig, and you'll get electrocuted." He glanced at Zeus and then Apollo again. "Maybe you should let *him* do it, just in case."

Apollo wouldn't have thought it possible given the dire circumstances, but he had to stifle a laugh at the look on Zeus's pucker. He shook his head. "I'll do it, but you better watch your back. My brother isn't looking too happy with you right now.

"Get over here, and tell me what to do." Although he didn't think it necessary at this point, he watched Sam as the man shuffled up to his side. "Don't make a mistake. My brother will see to it, it will be your last."

"I got it. Now pay close attention, this is *really* important: The keys are numbered so you need to make sure the right key goes into the correct lock." At Apollo's nod, he continued. "Okay, start with the third one first, then the fifth one second. Count to ten, do locks one and two in order, and then four. They will all open at the same time."

Apollo took a deep breath and inserted then turned the first of the keys and followed the instructions out until the locks popped open, and the gates began moving apart of their own accord. He blew out a small breath, relieved he was now one step closer to getting Isabella back.

Zeus came up next to them. "How many guards and where are they located?"

Sam's brows furrowed. "What day of the week is this?"

Apollo wanted to throttle him for stalling. "What difference does it make?"

"A lot. On weekends, there are only four outside guards. During the week, there can be as many as twenty guarding the grounds."

The vast difference in numbers didn't concern Apollo as much as the fact they were dealing with a weekday. But he needed to know everything before he put his brother and himself in danger. Isabella needed him alive, and his mother would want to kill him again if he died after promising not to. "How is it you don't know what day of the week it is?"

Sam shrugged. "When you're working for Mr. Barnabas, you are always on call. Days don't matter. Only seasons. Nobody hardly ever leaves the compound, definitely not without permission. Even the guards. It's just that during the week, they have to check every inch of their assigned part of the parameter, and this place goes deep into wooded lands that surround the cleared areas. Even I don't know how big it really is. On the weekends, they rotate who gets time off to stay at home to do whatever, and only the main building itself is guarded."

Apollo chewed on that for a moment. "How late do they work...the ones who guard during the week?"

Sam shrugged. "It varies, but most try to be home by dark. Although I doubt Mr. B knows that. He doesn't live here. He's just here now to take care of the Izzy issue. Once she was captured, we were supposed to leave immediately. He has another function to attend halfway across the country in a couple of days."

Vast relief accompanied a loudly expelled breath as Apollo exhaled. "So, if they've all gone home for the night by now, who is left?"

Sam's brows lifted, as if he understood he'd just delivered good news.

He smiled. "Only the four guarding the building."

"What's the routine?" Zeus asked, his voice filled with excitement.

Apollo grinned at his brother, understanding the nervous energy. It was building in him as well.

"They are stretched out somewhat evenly in distance," Sam continued, "and walk around the building for the entire shift. They stop at a certain point every fifteen minutes and report in. They keep in contact with each other with walky-talkies."

"Who do they report in to?" Apollo asked, itching to get moving.

"Each other. They used to report in to the switchboard. But the woman who ran it decided she wanted out after Mr. B made her marry one of the guards, and the guy beat her senseless." Sam eyed them warily for the first time in several minutes. "She got out, but not like she'd planned."

Apollo got the message. For now, he didn't have time to worry over anyone's murder, only the possibility of Isabella's. "Okay, do the guards know what goes on inside?"

As if surprised to be asked, Sam shook his head.

"I don't think so. Mr. B says people only know what he wants them to know, and most everything he deals in falls within a *need to know* category."

"So how do you know so much," Zeus asked, his voice laced with suspicion.

"Mr. B likes to conduct most of his business by phone while traveling from one facility or event to another." He smiled. "I have ears. And they work really well."

Ignoring Sam's attempt at levity, Apollo just nodded. "He's obviously got money. Why doesn't he fly?"

"He won't. I don't know why, but he won't."

Apollo stared at Sam, not sure what to do with him now. "What do you know about the inside? Do you know the layout of the building? Where they'd be holding Isabella?"

Sam shook his head. "I sit in the car unless Mr. B tells me to go away for a specific length of time. There's a little town on the compound. And a place where I can eat or, if he plans to stay more than the day, a small house with a room I can use to sleep in. I told you. This place is big."

"How far from here to the main building?" Zeus asked.

"Almost five miles, give or take."

Apollo slid a glance to Zeus. "What do you think?"

"I think he has to take a nap until we're done."

Sam looked back and forth between them, shaking his

head. "Please. I told you everything I know. I helped you!"

"He doesn't mean *kill* you," Apollo said, blandly.

Zeus shrugged. "I'm not opposed to it. He helped them take Isabella in the first place."

Apollo nodded, but unlike Zeus, he'd spent his life saving lives, not taking them. And unless it became necessary to do otherwise, he'd prefer it remain that way. "Sam, *old boy*, thanks for all your help," he said, before pulling his arm back and punching Sam hard in the jaw.

Sam's legs buckled, and he went down without a sound.

Zeus grinned as he reached down to lift the man over his shoulder and carry him back to the bed of the truck. Apollo met them there and applied a new length of tape to Sam's mouth, before covering him with a tarp from the bed's toolbox. That done, he and Zeus looked at each other.

"I'll race you," Zeus said, the light of the upcoming mission in his eyes.

Apollo laughed, in spite of the knots twisting his gut. "Get real."

Chapter Thirty-Two

Isabella kept her eyes closed, not because she was overly tired, which she was, but because they wouldn't turn off the lights, no matter how many times she'd asked early on. She'd given up trying to determine if anyone else was in the room, or listening in some other way, since there was never a response of any kind to her calls for help, unless one of those keeping her wanted to mock her from what she'd deduced was the open doorway. Even that had stopped after a while, once she heard the door snapping closed and no longer caught footsteps going up and down the hallway outside of the room.

Only recently learning to gauge time, it seemed hours to Isabella since anyone had actually come in to check on her, and that was fine by her. The last visitor had be the one they called Doc, and he'd done nothing but make her cry in humiliation when he'd had two other men come in to unstrap then hold her legs up and apart while he'd inserted what he'd called a catheter. Once her ankles were strapped down again, the doctor threw a blanket over her chilled body, as if he'd only just then realized how exposed she was. Thinking them done tormenting her, Isabella was surprised when one of the men appeared within her range of sight, grasped then turned her wrist and held it still, so an *intravenous line*, the doctor explained, could be inserted to drip some kind of liquid into her veins.

Isabella had watched his dispassionate face until he released her and stepped away. She listened for the footsteps indicating their departure, hating more than anything that she hadn't been able to move her head and see things for herself. When there were no sounds for what she felt a long period of time, she'd forced herself to relax, only then realizing whatever they were sending into her veins was making her feel oddly lightheaded. She struggled to fight whatever it was they were doing to her, determined more than ever not to give in and fall asleep.

She had no choice but to face what was really happening.

These people had no intention of letting her up, not even to go to the restroom. Were they only keeping her now to do as Sara had feared before she'd sent Isabella out of the compound? Was she only something for them to kill and dissect? Or worse, dissect while she was still alive? The tears flowing during the embarrassingly painful procedure she'd endured at the doctor's hands were nothing compared to the ones falling now. With so much despair in her heart, she was finally forced to gasp each breath through her mouth, as her nose was completely clogged.

It was hard believe her life had turned so sharply, not once, but twice in less than two weeks. There was a part of her that wished for the days of ignorance. If not bliss, at least she hadn't known how much in life there was to lose.

Then she'd think of all she'd learned, of all she'd experienced, of all those lives that had touched her with not only acceptance, but laughter, and love as well. She let the first kiss come back for the sweet memory it was, and most amazing, remembered the touch of Apollo from the first time they'd made hot and heavy love, until the last, when they'd laughed their way through it.

She would never know those things again.

Sadness burst into fury, and from fury to rage. Isabella opened her eyes and let it consume her, let it twist and turn inside. She let those happy memories loose and pulled the others closer. These people had stolen her life at the beginning of it! And now they'd stolen it again!

And she'd be *damned* if she'd lie like a slab of meat on a block and wait to be butchered!

Isabella closed her eyes again, this time letting Destiny's face be the one to form behind her eyelids, and the conversation they'd shared vibrate through her mind. *"You are very brave for one so young and inexperienced with life. You got away from them. You drove a great distance until you found us. You've embraced us without blinking an eye. And you are tackling your education head on, at great speed. A lesser person, if they'd even made it here, may have done nothing but tuck tail and hide."*

"Those aren't brave things. I just fell in love with you all. With your son. With the magic of your lives."

"Well, there you go. It takes bravery to hand over your heart to another, because there is nothing more dangerous than falling in love."

"I'm brave." Isabella whispered, determined to believe it. "I'm not a lesser person," she said a little louder. "I'm not going to hide!" she spouted, her confidence growing. "And I love you, wherever you are, Apollo Cavanaugh-Whitehawk, on purpose!" she shouted, as the joy of doing so set her free.

Tears formed in her eyes again, but she held them there, because she was *woman*, and no longer a child. "I'm brave, Apollo! I'm brave! Love is the most dangerous thing, and I still love you on purpose! And that makes me brave!"

The neck brace cracked in two, the wrist, belly, and ankle restraints snapped open. Alarms went off instantly, but she wasn't going to let them, or anything else, stop her from making her way back to her man.

Isabella reached over and jerked the IV out and then gritted her teeth as she reached down and did the same with the catheter. The pain she felt was nothing compared to the pain she would inflict on those who thought to make her their captive again.

She jumped from the bed and mentally fashioned a

toga with the thin blanket. The material submitted to her mind, as her feet raced to the door. Another thought undid the locks, and then she was in the same long hall she'd escape down before. Only this time there people running at her, guns being held out in front of them. Isabella threw up her hands, and their guns fell to the floor as their bodies flew to the ceiling where they hung like puppets on a string.

Isabella ran beneath them through the first of three sets of double doors she knew stood between her and freedom. She sent the second group of guards to the floor and stole their ability to move. Willing to embrace irony, since she was enjoying the endless flows of energy that now had been release, she sent their weapons to the ceiling and set them spinning.

The third corridor was empty, and her inner force spiked higher as her feet flew over the cold tiles. When Isabella made it to the exit she stopped and looked out, but there was no signs of life, so she took off, running into the night with all the strength her newfound bravery would afford.

She had to find Sara. She had to free her friend from the man who had abused her so badly. And they would need a car. Once they were together, they would escape the compound with all haste, because this time, Sara would *not* be left behind!

Isabella headed in the only direction she knew to take, running for all she was worth. It seemed to take forever, and she realized what had seemed a short distance, when driving or riding in the car all those times she and Sara had, was actually much longer on foot.

She finally made it, huffing so hard she could barely catch her breath as she studied the property she and Sara had shared. Illuminated by a single light at the top of the utility pole, the fenced in yard she'd once called a farm looked so much smaller than she remembered, the house much shabbier, and the land more dirt and weeds than lawn. Realizing she was comparing this desolate place once known as her home to what she'd found on Mystic Mountain, Isabella shook her head in wonder.

There *was* no comparison.

One was a real haven, a place of beauty well cared for by those who loved each other and their land. This place was exactly the opposite. No one cared for anything here, not even the value of a human life.

Of all the things she'd learned since first meeting Apollo, nothing matched the eye-opening lessons of being brought back to this place of horror, and to reality. Were it not for Sara's sacrifice, she herself would have never had a chance.

To live.

To love.

To know that beauty existed.

Isabella studied the house again, this time noticing there were no lights coming from within. Still winded, her side aching with a sharp pain, she made her way to it anyway, slowing down as she approached the front steps.

They'd never had air conditioning, so the open windows quickly revealed the house unoccupied. She made her way inside, taking the time to replenish her body with water from the tap, only to realize it wasn't as sweet and didn't satisfy her as the waters from Mystic Mountain did. With nothing else there for her, she headed out, and went in the direction she'd never tread.

The second house took some time to reach, and Isabella promised herself the first thing she'd learn when it came to lessons when she returned home, was how to figure distance. But she had to get there first. She hurried to the side of the house, and snuck around to peek in each window, horrified to finally catch sight of a sobbing Sara, who was bent over, holding her ankles, as she stood in the center of a small living room, and a long belt being swung before it smacked against her bloody bare bottom.

Isabella's fury resurfaced as rage, and she ran through the unlocked front door. Sara jerked around in surprise, and the leather of the next swing hit her face. Isabella's cry of distress caused the brute to spin around quickly. Before she could overcome her shock at the shape of her friend, he lashed out, and the large buckle hit her square in the temple.

Only a burst of disbelief flashed through Isabella, before everything went black.

Chapter Thirty-Three

The sight of the staff frozen on floors, and then hanging from the rafters, was the most precious sight Apollo had ever seen. Although he was certain the love of his life was the one who'd made jokes of those who'd meant to bring her harm, he and Zeus still ran through the building and checked every room. Coming up empty, they met back at the front door.

"Where would she have gone?"

Apollo frowned at Zeus. "She told me about her time here, how she lived with a woman named Sara, in a little house out on a farm. The only time she went anywhere was from that house to this building, and Sara, whoever she is, was kind enough to let Isabella drive what she called a short distance."

He thought about the stories she'd told, and almost smiled at the simplicity of her explanations at the very beginning. It would serve them both now. "I've got it! She said when she first went to live with Sara, and they'd head to what she'd always thought was her school, the sun always hurt her eyes, because, until then, she'd never been permitted to go outside." He glanced to the west, then back at Zeus. "I'm going after her. Contact the mothers and tell them where we are so they can come and help clean up this mess."

Zeus laid a hand on his arm. "Be careful, bro. We've got the building guards under control, and Isabella took care of those inside, but we don't know who's out there, between your woman and us."

Apollo nodded, his excitement renewed. "Yes, we do. I can take care of anyone I run into, by literally running into them before they realize what hit them. I aim to bring her home, brother, and I aim to do it immediately."

He took off at full hyper-speed and in seconds was at a dark little house much like the one Isabella had described. He made his way through it, disappointed, but determined to find some evidence he was on the right track.

There were no pictures, nothing to indicate a young girl had lived in the house, except when he finally glanced into the smaller bedroom's closet. Simple dresses, like the one Isabella had worn the day she'd landed on his mountain, hung in a neat little row.

Apollo touched one and then dropped it. Those homemade garments were a part of Isabella's past and wouldn't be a part of the future he wanted for them both. He quickly left the house and headed up the road.

The second house was dark as well, except for a faint bit of light shining through knee-high greenery that seemed to cover a small window at foundation level. Realizing it was possibly a basement, he hurried around the house twice, but there was no external entrance. Apollo approached quietly and lowered himself to his knees. He pushed tall grass and spiky weeds away, as he placed his head as close to the ground as he could to look in the narrow window.

Isabella!

Another woman was in there too. One who rocked back and forth over his beloved's prone body, crying hysterically. The fear that they'd killed Isabella before he could save her stole his breath and tore at his heart, and Apollo knew he'd tear the door down to get inside and kill whoever had done this! He started to raise his head, but the hard object that made his ears ring knocked him down completely before he blacked out.

Chapter Thirty-Four

Isabella awoke to ringing pain in her left temple, both ears, and even, it seemed, the roots of every one of her teeth. She lifted her hands and covered her ears, only it didn't help. It took several seconds to pinpoint the wailing cracking her skull wide open, even though it came from right above her head. "Sara, please stop!" she begged, barely able to speak over the nausea clawing at her throat.

"Izzy! Oh, Izzy! Dave said he'd killed you! I thought he'd killed you too!"

Isabella wasn't sure that wasn't the better option. She tried to move, to sit up, needing to get Sara out her face and somehow find a way to shut her up. In all the time they'd known each other, Sara had always been the adult. The reticent poster-child of calm. But right now, Isabella wanted to shout at her to stop acting like a child and pull it together. Time was precious. So priceless, if there was still a chance to escape. And since neither of them were dead yet, they had to honor that chance.

Yes, they both were injured *badly*, physically, emotionally, and she was concerned Sara mentally, but there was nothing they could do about that, other than help each other out in whatever way they could. More importantly, if that man thought her dead, it gave them opportunity. They needed get up and get moving. *Immediately*.

Pulling Sara's hands from her face, Isabella clasped it, and looked deeply into her eyes. "Sara, you've been my rock. My guardian angel. I need you to calm down and help me up."

The confusion in Sara's eyes was disheartening, but she finally nodded and took a shuddering breath. She backed away and slowly, awkwardly struggled to her feet. Isabella was worried she was too broken to make it out, but one way or another they both had to.

She rolled herself over, afraid Sara would be no help after all, and pushed at the floor until she was on her knees. Dizziness swamped her, and the matted mess of hair hanging in her face was a distraction, but as soon as she could sit back, that one, at least, could be handled quickly.

Isabella used both hands to pull the dull and dirty tresses away from her eyes, having little choice but to give her head a moment more to clear. She stretched her neck to the left, and then the right, stopping in mid-stretch to gasp in disbelief. Apollo was against the dirty concrete block wall. His arms stretched out to his sides and held in place by the chains, his head hanging down as blood seeped from beneath his ear and from the wound in his chest.

Just as she'd seen in her vision.

She crawled forward as hoarse moans of anguish overrode those of pain. She made it to his side, her palms and knees protesting, and used both his body and the cold wall to pull herself up before she cried out his name as both demand and prayer.

The vision was *wrong*. She was too late, Apollo was already dead!

Her breath caught as his head lifted, and that beautiful face looked at her with the same love her breaking heart held for him. When she leaned into him, he kissed her gently but with a sob, and then as if pulling on all his strength, with the passion she'd come to cherish.

"I will love you into eternity," he said, as a single tear flowed down his face. His head fell forward to hang limply, just as had happened in her vision.

Anguish tore through her anew, knowing what she'd find when she looked down his body. Spurts of blood pulsed out of the chest wound and ran rivers down his bare stomach and over the jeans he'd always worn so well. Knowing it futile, Isabella still went through the frantic motions of her vision, trying to stop the thick red flow, trying to pull the chains from the wall. But like before, she was sure he'd stopped breathing—and knew now, all was lost.

She cried out her anger, lost in her grief, not caring if it brought the killer to her. She'd lost everything that should have been her youth, but this was so much bigger…so very much more. If the one who had done this to the man she couldn't live without didn't take *her* life, too, she'd find a way to do it herself.

"*Isabella!*"

The commanding voice overrode her cries, as arms clasped her and attempted to pull her away. She fought to hold on to Apollo, knowing his shell was all she had left.

"Isabella! We have to hurry! Let go!"

Destiny's voice penetrated the grief buzzing in her head. Isabella looked up, lost in confusion, in disbelief, while she was viciously jerked from Apollo's side and held tightly in thick muscular arms. Apollo's mother and her sisters rushed forward, and Isabella watched in stunned disbelief as they magically released him, turned him into the blue faery dust, and whisked him away.

Chapter Thirty-Five

"Sara's asleep. Your mom, Rayne, and Haven are making sure her memories are as wiped away as her wounds. Sara should have the ability to start a new and much better life, so she never gives in to someone like Maximum Barnabas again."

Isabella frowned before continuing. "He got away. That monster wasn't even on the compound when your family swooped in to clean it out." She shook her head, hating that she'd let the despicable man's name leave her lips. "But I don't want to think about that right now."

Apollo smiled at her from the bed, holding out his hand in a silent request she join him. Isabella didn't need a second invitation. She climbed on and settled at his side. As always, she was amazed by the power of this extraordinary family but so thankful for it as well. Apollo was not only completely healed, he was hers to love on purpose once again.

Tears filled her eyes as she looked into his. "I thought I'd lost you."

To her surprise, his own eyes filled.

"I thought I'd lost *you*."

She smiled, her lips shaky, her heart overwhelmed that she'd found her way back home and into his arms. "Never again," she promised. "Never again."

THE END

Dear Readers,

Thank you for reading *Apollo: Unleashed*, book ten of the Cavanaugh series! I hope you enjoyed this book! There are still two more Cavanaugh stories to come before the last story, *Gavin's Ghost!* The horror Gavin White lived through as a child in Mystic Waters (in the first three books) has come back to haunt him as an adult. Now Gavin has lost everything again, for very different reasons. The last thing he needs is trouble when he moves back to Mystic Waters for his family's help, but… *But*, that's a story for another day! ;)

Mystic Waters Books
By JC Wardon

The Cavanaugh Series Books Now Available!
(The Cavanaugh Sisters Trilogy)
#1 **Mystic Thunder**
#2 **Touch of Lightning**
#3 **Tempest's Embrace**

(The Cavanaugh Series continues!)
#4 **Jewel of the Nile**
#5 **Sapphire Blues**
#6 **Diamond in the Rough**
#7 **Luna's Landing**
#8 **Celestial Liaison**
#9 **Zeus:** *Unbound!*
#10 **Apollo:** *Unleashed!*

The Cavanaugh Series Books to come!
Heracles: Undone
Soleli's Secret
Gavin's Ghosts

Blood Moon Chronicles
Blood Moon Rising

Visit my website: **www.jcwardon.com**, Facebook pages:
www.facebook.com/jc.wardon and
https://www.facebook.com/JCWardonNovelist and
tweet me: @jc_wardon.

Thanks for sharing my world. I'd love to hear from you!

JC Wardon

While you await the next Cavanaugh release, I hope you'll check out the start of my new series, the *Blood Moon Chronicles*! The first novel: **Blood Moon Rising** is available now!

Visit my website: **www.jcwardon.com**, my Facebook pages: **www.facebook.com/jc.wardon** and **https://www.facebook.com/JCWardonNovelist** and tweet me: @jc_wardon

Thanks for sharing my world. I'd love to hear from you! And… if you'd like a little taste of *Heracles*… Check out the following pages!

JC Wardon

Heracles: *Undone!*

Prologue

Heracles lifted his chin and tilted his head *just so*, envisioning the photographic results of his pose as the late morning's breeze blew through his sun-streak-resistant black hair. The still rising sun sent strong beams to bounce off his chiseled physique. The Mediterranean's cool waters hit the rocks, at just the right angle to spray at his back and against his nearly bare ass and honed thighs. A still photo, with water droplets hanging up in the air and around him, was the immediate goal, but it had to be accomplished without the ocean's water messing up his hair. That ship was going to sail soon if the photographer didn't hurry.

He'd been in the game long enough to know the pose showed off his strong Whitehawk features to his best advantage, as well as emphasizing the bulging package beneath the tight scraps of material the agency had sent him here to hawk. He almost snorted out a laugh at the thought of hawking his wares as if he were some two-bit whore, but it wasn't all that far from the truth. As a professional model, he *was* selling his body as much as the clothing they dressed him in—or in this case, the lack of it. One was for the purchasing public, and the other, *himself*, was for the designers who wanted him specifically to show off their newest designs.

Today he'd sold himself to Miles Titan, owner and CEO of Titan Body Wears. For the past three days, he'd modeled men's workout wear, designer scuba attire, and this morning, the bathing suit line. After his long overdue vacation, which started as soon as the photographer called them done, he'd do the same for some other designer, at some other local, but the endgame was always the same. Get a sexual-sensory response from those who saw the magazine ads, so they'd be enticed to buy the swimwear. Or underwear. Or whatever type of clothing Heracles contracted, to hook the masses of women who wanted their men to look just like him when similarly clothed.

There was never a doubt in his mind what the target audience was. And he was nothing more to any of them than eye-candy to hum over and fantasize about.

His life as male supermodel was apparently losing its luster, Heracles mused, as he moved and then settled into the next pose without direction. He'd worked with this photographer several times over the years, and though the man took a great picture, he had little imagination when it came to directing a shoot. If both of them weren't being paid ridiculous amounts of money, and Heracles wasn't being catered to in the most luxurious accommodations this island had to offer, he'd give into the temptation to flip the cameraman off and take a reviving dive and swim into the deep waters just below the bolder he was posed upon. But that would wet down his hair and actually get the suit wet, which then wouldn't photograph the way the client wanted.

It was chilly, standing in the surf winds this morning, but the renowned photographer wanted just the right mixture of shadows and sun on his breeze-tossed hair. The rising fiery ball in the sky would reflect well off Heracles' genetically perfect tan. He was glad his Whitehawk and Cavanaugh genes didn't allow the lack of sleep and partying too hard the night before to affect his features in any way, as it had the women who were supposed to have been on this shoot, too. They'd both gotten a serious scolding by the make-up artists and Jose Declodes, the head of the talent agency, and were now back in the hotel packing to leave.

Heracles felt bad for them and knew he should have warned them about how his ability to play all night and keep functioning just fine might affect them differently. He *hadn't* given it a thought, but then, his life was so easy, so breezy, he rarely thought beyond the moment.

"Whitehawk! You falling asleep up there?"

"Sorry!" he yelled back and struck the next pose.

"Now pull your bathing suit down off your hips with your thumbs and hold it so it covers the root of your penis, but just barely."

Heracles did as instructed, shrugging mentally rather than rolling his eyes. This had become his signature pose whether with swimwear, underwear, or hip-gloving jeans, and every photographer had to get one in.

"That's a wrap!"

Relieved, and ready to hit the hotel and the bed for a few hours, Heracles pulled up the swim suit and looked over to see the makeup artists and camera crews packing up quickly. Everyone had been up and at it since before dawn, and the *wrap* was welcomed by all. He headed to the rocks, where he'd left his robe and boat shoes, and stopped short when he noticed the long, lean, casually dressed man sitting next to his things. There was a lot about the man that was out of place, but the oddest was the cowboy hat held in his large hand, and the silver-tipped boots on his feet.

Miles Titan?

Heracles had heard the elusive designer would be at the shoot and had actually dreaded it. This designer was an unknown among his contacts, and persons outside of modeling circles who stood around during a shoot often caused disasters in one way or another. Either because of distraction or the inability to stay out of the way and leave everyone alone, bystanders were never really welcomed.

Especially when it came to those who had hired the lot of them. *They* always had opinions, offered unwanted input, and sometimes even completely changed the direction of an ongoing shoot while in the midst of it. Today, this man hadn't done any of that.

That hadn't been the case originally.

Weeks before, when the job offer first came to his attention, Titan's spokesperson stipulated the model representing the swim and diving wear had to *look* like a man's man, body hair and all. Since he'd wanted the shoot, and he normally kept his body waxed from eyebrows to toes, Heracles had had to endure the itching of letting it all grow back in after years of keeping himself groomed to the max. At first he'd been irritated, but he had to admit he actually looked pretty good with both facial and body hair, the biggest bonus being he actually looked closer to his age.

The fact that he hadn't physically changed since around his twenty-first year was great for business, but it caused people to treat him as if he had little life experience. Which, he had to admit, held a degree of truth. A life of being fawned over and catered to hadn't toughened him up as it had his identical triplet brothers. But he could still take a punch from either of them and give back just as good. Which was something to look forward to since he was finally going home for a while.

Heracles made his way to the rocks slowly and looked the man over again. The visitor didn't seem too happy. Was he mad because he'd been ignored? Didn't like what he'd seen? Or had been kept waiting too long? If this *was* Miles Titan, he'd done nothing more today than sit on the sidelines and watch the show. Heracles wasn't used to clients not liking the results of his shoots, so he hoped he wasn't about to find out this trip has been a waste of time.

Either way, he got paid, but it was the principle of the thing. He had a name and brand to uphold too. Although, that was becoming a problem all its own.

The guy stood and placed the hat on somewhat shaggy blond hair. As Heracles reached him, a work-roughened hand held out the hotel's robe.

"Thanks. I'm Heracles Whitehawk."

"I know who you are. I'm Greg Gains, here on Miles Titan's behalf."

Not letting his surprise show, Heracles slipped into the robe. He pulled it closed and knotted the sash before nodding. "Nice to meet you. I was told the designer would be here."

"Miles couldn't make it, so I'm here to make the offer. You want to get some breakfast?"

Heracles blinked but tried not to react otherwise. *What offer? Another shoot opportunity?* The news was disheartening. He'd been working nearly nonstop for the past year, and the long planned break wasn't something he was willing to give up.

Since the designer had taken him on for this particular shoot, there was a degree of obligation, *and* he was always hungry.

One did not eat much on a regular basis, certainly not filling foods like carbs, when one wanted to look as he did. His body was his bread and butter, which required he avoid both bread *and* butter, as often as possible. Even though he would turn down whatever offer this man came to deliver, there was no harm in hearing him out. And it beat the hell out of sitting in the restaurant alone. "I could eat."

What looked like sun-aged lines bracketed the hint of grin the newcomer sent his way. Heracles let the thought register that the man should have used sunblock, as it was clear he spent a great deal of time out in the sun. Which made little sense, since he obviously worked for the designer.

Heracles knocked the sandy soil from his feet and slid

on his shoes, as his stomach growled. "They have a great buffet in the hotel's main restaurant. I'd planned to try it out once the shoot was over. Now that it is, I'm likely to hit it hard."

Greg nodded. "You could use a little more meat on your bones."

Heracles stopped in the process of stepping off the rock, a frown on his face. "I'm sorry?"

"It wasn't an insult, just an observation. I'm learning. You model types tend to starve yourselves. It looks great on film, I guess. But must be hard to sustain."

Somewhat mollified and noticing Greg was a little buff for a guy who worked in the industry, Heracles nodded slowly. "It can be. The only time I ever overindulge is right after a shoot or when my large family all gets together to chow down. Unless I have a shoot coming up, right after a family get-together. Even then probably, but I work out like a demon to make sure it doesn't show."

Greg looked him over, his gaze assessing. "You're what the boss wants. Which is why I'm here. I have a proposition for you."

Heracles hesitated. The last thing he wanted to do was insult an industry insider. But if Miles Titan sent this man to offer anything but work, he was barking up the wrong tree. "What kind of proposition?"

Heracles stepped down from the bolder a rock at a time and then waited as Greg jumped down and landed hard, his boots kicking up the sand.

Greg cleared his throat. "We'll get into that. But I'm tired and hungry. Let's get some food."

Uneasy air hung between them as they crossed the beach and made the long walk up the wooden boardwalk leading to the rear entrance of the large hotel. The design and style of both building and garden-enhanced pool area blended in perfectly with the island's Mediterranean location and feel. Though somewhat new, the luxurious vacation resort looked as if built centuries before. When they reached the entrance Heracles stopped, debating demanding answers before they shared a meal.

If Miles Titan sent this man to procure Heracles as a lover, then he would have to make it clear he wasn't gay, *again*. He'd heard and read the recent rumors, knowing them started by a couple of the women he'd modeled with and then rejected later, when they'd wanted to be linked romantically with him. The publicity alone could elevate their own careers, because Heracles had long been considered an elusive goldmine to be harvested in their world.

It was embarrassing, but it was more important to keep his family safely out of the spotlight. That was the only reason he hadn't had more than casual flings throughout his career. Having tired of that, he'd chosen celibacy for the past year. It hadn't always been easy, but not all that hard either. Not having to perform nightly, when his heart wasn't in it, seemed the best decision he'd made in a long time.

Until now.

Two of the rejected were coming back to bite him in the ass. Both Doral and Katrina had threatened him with bad publicity when he'd sent them on their way without sex following last month's runway shows. They'd banded together to make their lies look like truth, and Heracles was afraid, now that this ball was rolling, others would see the benefit of jumping on to make matters even worse.

He had no doubt they were thrilled to make all the tabloids. He wasn't. But there wasn't a damned thing he could do about it. To debate the issue publicly would only add more fuel to a fire he wanted to die. *Before* reporters and cameramen started showing up on Mystic Mountain to get answers to what had suddenly become one of media's biggest questions.

Heracles knew he hadn't looked tough in the way some men did when he'd kept himself waxed. Staying well groomed was just part of the job, something he'd grown accustomed to and gave no real thought to. The most irritating part was it shouldn't have even been an issue, as it should make no difference to anyone, either way. Many of his best friends in the industry were gay, both models and designers. But the tabloids were eating it up and making his sexuality fodder for the public to chew on and spit out. That, more than anything, was why he needed a break so badly. He had to hide until the furor died down.

"You change your mind about eating?"

Heracles shook his head. "No. Just thinking. I'll get dressed and be right back down." Greg opened his mouth, closed it, and then nodded as his brows knitted. "You worried about something?"

"No. Of course not."

"Then what is it?"

"I'm not gay."

Looking truly uneasy, Greg shrugged. "Didn't say you were."

Heracles nodded but felt no better. "I'll be ten minutes." Greg's frown made it clear he thought Heracles odd, when in fact he was just getting more confused.

"I'll get us a table by the pool."

"I'll be quick, then."

Heracles hurried inside, wondering what in the world was going on. He knew his family thought he was shallow, to the point of blatant ignorance when it came to reading other people, but that wasn't true. He'd either disappointed Greg with his declaration or had offended the man somehow.

Nearly twenty minutes later, clean, dressed casually, and feeling like an idiot, Heracles made his way back to the patio, expecting to find Greg long gone. But he wasn't. He was sipping what looked like a large cup of coffee and waving the waiter off. His relieved smile appeared when he spotted Heracles.

"Sorry. That took longer than I expected."

Greg shrugged. "No problem."

"Thanks. I appreciate the duds." Heracles grinned. "You have to love a job where you get to keep all the great clothes you model. These are so breezy and comfortable, especially for this climate."

Greg tilted his head, looking Heracles over with a critical eye. "Not everyone does. Get to keep the clothes, that is. Miles says you're special."

Heracles didn't know how to respond. He knew he got *perks* many others in the industry didn't, but Greg's comment seemed more personal. He shrugged. "I do try to give designer types what they want."

Greg's lips twitched. "Designer types?"

Heracles grinned. "Yeah. As in, clothes masters."

"Ah. I see."

The cross look was pulling his brows together again, and Heracles knew he'd have to hit this conversation head on. "Look, man. I think Miles Titan is a great beachwear designer, especially to be so new. These clothes will sell themselves, with anyone modeling them."

Greg shrugged. "I'll have to take your word for it. The waiter is waiting for me to signal him to come over."

Heracles stared at the man across from him, dumbfounded. Since when did a designer's rep not have a clue about the product or the industry? "What's really going on here?"

Greg studied Heracles and then exhaled loudly. "I'm just here to make the offer and fly you back to the ranch if you accept."

Heracles snapped his mouth closed when he realized it

was hanging open. He didn't know what to ask first, so he threw questions out as they came. "What offer? What ranch? Where?"

Greg settled back as the waiter approached. He turned to the man and shook his head. "Give us another minute."

The waiter backed away, and Greg looked Heracles over and shook his head. "You sure do look different than the man in the magazines Miles keeps. Made me wonder why you were the top choice. But now you look rougher, older, and your coloring is dead on, although you could use a little scuffing up. Guess I should trust Miles knows what's what when it comes to this stuff."

He sighed. "I don't know what you usually do, or get for doing it, but this offer is legit. A couple of months on Miles' ranch, modeling a western wear line being developed. It's a new concept for the boss, so you'll be there from start to finish. The line is still in the designing stages, and Miles wants yours as the body to design on and for, although we may need to feed you a little more first."

For the first time, Greg laughed. "You've got the muscles but could use a little more bulk, or the boys are going to eat you alive. Once the clothes are finished, you'll be the only model for the entire campaign. It's top secret, and no one is to know you are involved, or even that Miles is starting this new line, until it's made public at Fall Fashion Week in New York. I have the contract with me for you to look over. But we're scheduled to fly out in a couple of hours, so you need to decide quickly."

The waiter sat a tall glass of juice before Heracles. "Excuse me, sirs. Have you decided yet?"

Heracles nodded, still clueless, but intrigued by the idea of losing himself on some out-of-the-way ranch for a while. He had no idea what to think about *the boys* who might eat him alive, but he'd table that for later. He spoke to the waiter, not taking his eyes off Greg. "I'll have the buffet."

"I'll have the same."

The waiter left immediately, and Heracles took a drink of his orange juice to wet his dry mouth. "I guess you'd better hand the contract over."

Greg remained silent while Heracles read the document. He reread it again after filling his plate and while eating. He usually would have Amanda, his agent, handle everything, but the terms were simple and straightforward, and not including her, until it came time for payment, would make him that much harder to find.

When he looked up and nodded, Greg reached into his shirt pocket and pulled out a folded check before sliding it across the table.

"This is the advance."

Heracles didn't unfold it, as the staggering amount was spelled out in the contract. He wouldn't touch the money until everything was said and done. If Amanda weren't so thrilled with all the recent publicity, he'd include her in his change of plans now. Thankfully, she'd think him on the vacation he'd insisted on and wouldn't really expect him to answer even if she called. He'd make sure she got her commission on the job as always, but he needed this escape, with none the wiser. And that included his agent.

"I'll need to pack."

Greg nodded. "The car is waiting out front." He hesitated. "There's just one more thing."

Heracles rose, and waited. "What?"

"Miles is like family to me."

When Greg said no more, Heracles nodded and headed for his room...wondering why those few words felt like a warning of some kind.

Happy Reading! JCW

ABOUT JC WARDON

JC Wardon loves writing fantasy and spends her days weaving stories for those who love it as well. Though she has great appreciation for romances, a juicy and complicated plot is what she holds most dear. Danger, mystery, and magic are the life's blood for her Mystic Waters Books. She hopes you are captivated and stimulated, and your hearts become engaged.

If you enjoyed *Apollo: Unleashed,* please consider telling others and writing a review.

WWW.JCWARDON.COM